VALLEY OF THE RATS

MAHTAB NARSIMHAN

We acknowledge financial support for our publishing activities: the Government of
Canada, through the Canada Book Fund and The Canada Council for the Arts;
the Government of Ontario, through the Ontario Arts Council, Ontario Creates,
and the Ontario Book Publishing Tax Credit. We acknowledge additional funding
provided by the Government of Ontario and the Ontario Arts Council
to address the adverse effects of the novel coronavirus pandemic.

LIBRARY AND ARCHIVES CANADA CATALOGUING IN PUBLICATION

Title: Valley of the rats / Mahtab Narsimhan.
Names: Narsimhan, Mahtab, author.
Identifiers: Canadiana (print) 20210211911 | Canadiana (ebook) 20210211938 |
ISBN 9781770866287 (softcover) | ISBN 9781770866294 (HTML)
Classification: LCC PS8627.A77 V35 2021 | DDC jC813/.6—dc23

United States Library of Congress Control Number: 2021938483

Cover art: Nick Craine
Interior text design/rat illustration: Tannice Goddard, tannicegdesigns.ca

Printed and bound in Canada.
Manufactured by Friesens in Altona, Manitoba in August, 2021.

DCB
An imprint of Cormorant Books Inc.
260 Spadina Avenue, Suite 502, Toronto, ON M5T 2E4
www.dcbyoungreaders.com
www.cormorantbooks.com

For Barry

CHAPTER 1

The night a rat bit my butt was my lucky night. I just didn't know it at the time.

Our GPS was busted, there had been no cellphone signal since we left camp, and we were lost. Dad, optimistic as ever, said we had to keep going till we reached a small town or village. I didn't want to remind him that he'd said that three hours ago. The hand sanitizer I kept in my pocket had fallen out someplace, but Dad didn't want to stop while I took out the backup from my camping gear. Desperate to get into a warm tent before I froze to death, I tried to keep up.

I'd tried the radio several times within the past hour, but it was spewing nothing except static. The forest of bamboos surrounding us must have been the reason. Thirty feet tall, they seemed to be natural barriers to any kind of radio or cell signal.

"Isn't this fantastic?" Dad said, striding on. "You, me, and the great outdoors."

With all this bamboo around me, it felt more like being trapped in a large cage.

We'd left the main campsite over a day ago. There were a gazillion germs on me, but I tried to get a grip on my panic and plodded on behind Dad. There were germs at home, and I'd survived. I would survive this too — if I kept my head and found the hand sanitizer as soon as we stopped.

"Dad, it's almost dark," I said, glancing at the luminous dial of my watch. "Let's stop for the nigh—AHHH!"

A shadow, close enough to touch, zipped through the dense bamboo.

"Who's that?" I squeaked.

Dad came crashing back. "Was it a person or an animal?"

I stared into the darkness till spots danced in front of my eyes. Nothing moved. "I'm not sure."

"Can you describe it?" said Dad, gripping my shoulders. "Close your eyes and think carefully."

We were hungry, lost, cold, and filthy. Dad was *excited*?

"Dad, it was a large shadow. I couldn't make out much."

"What if we looked around for a minute —" Dad started to say.

I cut him off. "Can we please find a campsite and stop for the night? I'm beat." I tried not to sound whiny, but I knew I did. What had I been *thinking*, begging to go on an outdoor trip? A trip to the grocery store made me want to don a hazmat suit.

Dad sighed and started walking. He didn't have to say it, but I knew he was disappointed and trying not to be too obvious about it. He had no idea I could pick up a tone, a gesture, a look, and interpret it accurately. Especially his. I'd had years of practice.

"Chin up, Krish. Things will be better in the morning. Let's find a good spot to put up the tents. I'll get a fire going, and we'll have a hot meal. Okay?"

"Okay."

I gazed at Dad's broad back. I'd thought this trip would help us to understand each other, to bond. Instead, it had shown me just how different we were. Was there any point in even trying?

The forest was alive, and my neck hurt from constantly looking around. The wind howled overhead like someone in pain. A hoot punctuated the incessant scurrying and clicking. I started, my eyes scanning the impenetrable darkness. Did owls attack humans? Was that slithering sound a snake beside me?

Someone was watching us. It was a gut feel (GF) — sometimes a cold breeze on the back of my neck and sometimes a severe stomach ache. Right now, I had the pleasure of both.

I wished I could confide in Dad, but he believed in facts, not feelings. GFs had been the reason for countless arguments on this trip. I admit, sometimes my imagination soared.

Not this time. Someone was following us.

We hiked uphill through the tall bamboo. The temperature plummeted. I switched on the headlamp and followed the beam of light as I put one aching foot in front of the other. I focused on breathing deeply and promised myself that if I got out of this alive, I would think of some other way to bond with Dad. Maybe a *National Geographic* documentary would be more my style. He might enjoy it too.

"Need a breather, Dad!" I plopped down on a rock — and leaped right back up again. "Ow!" I said, twisting to look at the sharp rock I'd sat on.

I wished it had been a rock. It turned out to be a white rat with sharp teeth and a red snout, still hanging off my butt. Screaming, I swiped at it. It squeaked and zipped into the bushes. Panic ballooned, making it hard to breathe or talk.

"What happened?" said Dad, racing to me.

My hand shook as I pointed to the shadowy forest. "Rat bit me. I can feel the poison spreading, and I'll be dead soon. Bye, Dad. Tell Mom I love her."

Dad hugged me tight. "Shhh, Krish. Deep breaths. There's no way such a small rat could chew through your thick pants in a second. Let me have a look."

His soft tone and warm hug made me want to bawl. I hadn't realized how much I'd needed this. It had taken a *near-death experience* to get him to soften up. I focused on pulling air into my lungs while Dad examined my butt.

He turned me around and squatted. "Krish, there's just the *slightest* tear in your pants. It didn't reach skin. You're safe from rabies or any other disease the rat might have had. You'll outlive me, son."

"You're sure about that? No blood?"

"Nope," said Dad.

"Okay." I let out a shaky breath.

"Now, let's find a sheltered place and set up the tent," said Dad, patting my shoulder. "You're handling this quite well, Krish. You'll feel better after a couple of hot dogs and a good night's sleep."

"Okay," I mumbled, ashamed of my panic. If you thought about it, a rat biting my butt was *hilarious*. It would make a great story. Except, I didn't feel like laughing. "I wish I could be as comfortable as you are out here. But I'm not," I said, staring at him. "I don't think I'll ever be."

"Argue for your limitations and they're yours," said Dad. "Consider this is an adventure story you're living instead of reading. You took the first step in asking to go on this trip, and I'll help you get through it. Okay?"

If I spoke now, I'd probably cry. *At least it's not raining*, I thought. Right on cue, lightning split the sky, followed by a loud clap of thunder. The deluge began.

Fantastic.

Aching all over, I trudged behind Dad, our headlamps cutting twin swathes of light through the darkness. The smell of wet earth and rotting leaves filled the air. I still couldn't shake the feeling someone was watching us. Friend, foe, or wild animal?

Four pinpricks of light glowed in the undergrowth. I trained my headlamp on the spot and shuddered. "Dad," I said, grabbing the back of his jacket.

"Krish?" he replied, wearily.

"Two rats are staring at me."

"We're in the wilderness. Did you expect puppies?"

The rats were large, black, and hairy. The white one, who'd tried to sample my butt, had disappeared. My brain, brimming with trivia, supplied an interesting one: rats were carnivores and cannibalistic.

Surprisingly, the rats didn't look scared of us. They watched us with their beady eyes, and I swear they spoke to each other in rat-chitter. I tried not to think of the germs swarming on them and went to my happy place: at my desk, in my clean room, reading a book while I munched on my fave snacks — chips and candies.

"Shoo!" I yelled as one of them approached us, its nose twitching.

"Krish, don't. No point yelling and alerting anyone else to our presence."

"You mean there's something dangerous out here?" I managed to choke out the words.

Dad shrugged. "I've heard some odd rumours about the Ladakh Range, but seeing is believing. Getting a picture is money in the bank." He chuckled.

Dad was a nature photographer, always chasing the exciting, the unknown. The more bizarre the subject or habitat, the keener he was to photograph it.

"How can you even think of a picture when our lives may be in danger?"

"We're safe, Krish, only lost. You can't get any of this from a book or computer. I want to give you a chance to see our amazing world for real."

"What's wrong with books or the internet?" I asked, pressing my advantage. "You can learn so much. Ask me anything — go on."

"Reading about lighting a fire and actually doing it are very different," said Dad, walking on.

"That's what a lighter or flints are for," I said.

"What if you lose your flints and matches and have to rely on the forest? You remember that fun movie with Tom

Hanks marooned on an island? What was it?" said Dad, snapping his fingers, trying to remember. "He'd named a football Mr. Wilson."

"*Castaway*," I said. That was a horror movie, not a fun adventure.

"Right," said Dad. "Hanks had to make fire using his brains and what was available on the island. You have to make do with what you have and dig deep when things go south. It's called survival."

I got what Dad was trying to do, but how could I make him understand that I would never appreciate the real thing? Not when it scared me so much. This trip, so far, ranked highest on my to-avoid list, higher than touching the handle of a grocery cart or a bathroom doorknob. And yet, I'd *made* the effort. Could he not see how hard this was for me and at least give me some credit for trying?

The rats interrupted my black thoughts with squeaks and clicks. They disappeared into the undergrowth as soon as our headlamps shone on them.

"Hopefully they won't come back," said Dad, swiping the rain off his face. "Let's camp here tonight and get our bearings in the morning. As soon as we get a signal, I'll radio Adventure Camp and tell them to send a guide to lead us back. Okay, Krish? You'll be back with your cousin Anjali before you know it."

"Thanks, Dad." I'd take Anjali over the rats. What Dad didn't know was that getting away from Anjali was the reason I'd agreed to break from Adventure Camp to go on this side trip.

A bit of trivia popped into my head, and bizarre as it was, I knew it was the right thing to do. "Let's follow the rats," I said. One more night in the forest would kill me. I longed to pop a candy into my mouth, but I'd wait till I'd fished my hand sanitizer out of my backpack.

"Are you okay?" Dad placed a grimy hand on my forehead, and I flinched. "You want to follow *rats*?"

"They're nocturnal creatures," I replied. "They hunt for food at night. Where there's food, there are people. And houses and a phone."

"I'm impressed," said Dad, hefting his backpack and camera case higher on his shoulders. "That's very useful information. Let's go."

My heart glowed, and the chill lessened. I didn't want to ruin this moment by gloating that I'd read that fact in a book.

We followed the rats further uphill. A couple of times, we lost them, but they squeaked, letting us know where they were. It was as if they wanted us to keep following them. I'd never read or heard of this type of rat behaviour, but I filed it away to research as soon as I got back.

Branches slapped my face. I muttered a choice f-word.

Frittata!

An owl hooted. Another answered. An almost-full moon peeped from behind a ragged cloud. It grew colder, and my breath fogged, but my pits dripped sweat. What if we were making a mistake following the rats? What if something happened to Dad, and I was left all alone? What if that mystery shadow attacked us? I tried to push the thoughts away and stared up at the sky through the bamboo. The darkness was pierced by millions of silver pinpoints.

A horrible smell hit my nose — a mix of rotting meat and feces. "What's that stink?"

"Dead animal," said Dad.

My skin sizzled as if electrocuted. More germs. I held out my hands in the rain till they seemed clean, sort of, and popped a candy into my mouth. I chewed slowly, deliberately. As I counted backwards from a hundred, my heartbeat slowed.

"Do you see the rats?" Dad called out, peering into the bushes beside him. "They're gone."

We had been climbing uphill, and my legs ached. Nothing moved except silver slashes of rain. Those dirty rats had led us here and disappeared. Not a claw or tail in sight. Only a dense line of trees and the sound of the wind whooshing through empty space.

"No people and no food," said Dad. "Guess that little fact

didn't work out, Krish." He slid his large backpack off and groaned, massaging his shoulders.

I tried not to let my disappointment show. I had been so sure of my facts, but out here, I was as good as useless. And now Dad knew it too.

The tree cover was thin, and I felt every jab and bite of wind on my face. "Maybe we could try the radio up here?" I said. "See if we can get a signal."

"If that makes you happy," Dad said and fished out the radio. I couldn't be sure if he was being sarcastic or concerned. I was too tired to care. I'd made a huge mistake, and I wanted this to be over.

"Kabir Roy to Adventure Camp. My son, Krish, and I are lost, and our GPS and cellphones aren't working. We're a day and a half trek from Leh, somewhere in the Ladakh Range. We need a guide to lead us back to camp. Over and out."

Only the rain and wind spoke.

"May I try?" I said.

Dad handed me the radio. I tried once more, sweeping all the frequencies. On an impulse, I switched to the frequency that Anjali and I used when we'd go on family camping trips. She'd be in her tent with her mom and dad. I'd be in mine. We'd switch on our radios and chat late into the night — about everything and nothing.

"This is Krish! Can you hear me?" I stopped short of

saying *Anjali*. If she was listening, she would know. But would she answer, after the way I'd let her down last summer?

Nothing. I clipped the radio on to my belt, making a mental note to check the battery as soon as we were out of the rain.

"We should have pitched a tent when we were lower down," said Dad. "The wind is too strong here, and we'll freeze. Let's go back."

His flat tone made me sick. I walked away, searching the thick tangle of roots for a glimpse of the rats. The stink was stronger here, and I took shallow breaths. Facts are facts. The rats had to be close by. My GF said they were. And not only rats. Something or someone else. Much bigger than the rats.

My pulse raced as I stared at a thick clump of bushes. A shadowy figure squatted low to the ground.

"Who's there?" I whispered.

A gruff voice said, "Run!"

CHAPTER 2

I obeyed without argument, crashing through the bushes, yelling for Dad. My arms and legs were pumping so hard, I overshot him. He grabbed me and pulled me back. "Krish! Did you see the rats again?"

I held on to him, trying to breathe.

"It's okay, I'm here," said Dad, holding me close. "You're safe."

"Something in the forest told me to run," I said.

Dad's headlamp shone directly in my eyes. I squinted.

"What do you mean something told you? There's no one here but us and rats. I don't think rats can speak."

I described what I had seen and heard.

"Show me."

I led him back to the spot, my heartbeat so loud in my ears that it drowned out the howling wind. We searched every bush in the vicinity. Nothing.

"They're gone now," I said. "It *wasn't* my imagination."

"I'm sorry, Krish," Dad said, scrubbing his face. "This was

too ambitious a trip for you. We should have stayed at the Adventure Camp with Naveen and Anjali." Disappointment made his voice flat. Almost uncaring. "Your cousin Anjali would have loved this. She's the adventurous sort."

There it was again — the unrelenting comparison between Dad's niece, Anjali, and me. She loved the outdoors. and always came out looking good. I *always* fell short.

"Let's find a place to camp," I said, trying not to let him see how much I was hurting.

My GF tingled. Cold breeze, check. Stomach ache, check. I walked back up toward the edge of the tree line. My heart raced, knowing I was steps away from a steep drop. One strong gust of wind and it was goodbye world.

I shuffled up to where the bushes thinned and peered out into the sea of darkness. A glimmer, way down, caught my eye.

"*Dad!* Over here!"

Dad hurried back up and saw where I was pointing. Light flickered down below — probably a village. And where there's a village, there are four walls and a roof, a place to shower and have a hot meal … yessss!

"Saved!" said Dad, thumping me on the back. "Good call following the rats, and well spotted, Krish."

The weight from my shoulders lifted. *Well spotted, Krish.* Did I dare tell him it was thanks to my GF that I'd stopped to take a look? Something told me now was not a good time.

To get to the village in the valley, we had to scramble down the steep mountainside. The descent was barf-inducing. Dad took the lead. I followed, taking care to step exactly where he did. The moon and our headlamps lit the slope, which was pockmarked with craters and debris the size of soccer balls. Some twice that. Certain sections were sheer rock.

Don't let me fall became my mantra at every step.

As we descended, the foul stink grew and mingled with a faint smell of onions and woodsmoke. *Rattus rattus* returned, with friends. Five of them sat at a distance, staring at us.

I climbed down cautiously — a foot, then a hand at a time. My body trembled with the exertion. Turning the pages of a book or typing was my idea of cardio. *This* was like asking a toddler to run a marathon.

The mountainside was slick with rain, and I slipped despite the rubber grips on my boots. My hands were chafed and raw as I clung to the rocks. Down we went, agonizingly slowly.

Step down, move hand, breathe. Over and over till my muscles screamed in agony.

The glimmer grew stronger. We were almost there. I could do this. I was going to do this!

Suddenly my handhold of rock crumbled and fell away.

"Dad!" I yelped as I grabbed a nearby bush and slammed against the rock face.

I felt a crunch. Ribcage or hip bone? I waited for pain to blossom. Nothing. I clung to the mountain face, gulping in air.

Dad was immediately by my side, supporting me. "I can't do this in the dark," I said in a shaky voice. "I'm so sorry, but I can't. Please, let's wait for morning." I was ashamed that I was blabbering, but I was at the end of my strength, and I didn't care what he thought of me.

Dad clung beside me with one arm, the other encircling my shoulders. "You've done a fantastic job so far, Krish. I'm so impressed with how you've handled this descent with no prior training."

"Really?" I asked, my pulse slowing a bit.

"Yes. We're almost to the bottom. The villagers are sure to have a phone or radio. We'll call for help, and before you know it, you'll be back home. Can you be brave a *little* while longer?"

I swallowed my tears. Twelve was too old to cry, and I would never forgive myself for bawling. I glanced at the village below, its glowing huts shaped in concentric circles around a clearing. There lay food, warmth, and safety.

I'd read about athletes digging deep for endurance and finding it, even though they felt they couldn't go on. Though

I wasn't an athlete, I'd reach all the way to my toes to find the strength to get down this mountain. Dad had said he was impressed, and I wasn't going to do anything to spoil that.

"I see an easier way, Krish. Follow me."

We inched over to a section sheltered by an outcrop of rock. It was drier, and the descent was quicker now that I had a better grip on the steep slope. The lower we went, the louder the sounds of scurrying feet. I couldn't see the rats, but I could hear them. I forced myself to think of puppies. *Pudgy, golden retriever puppies.*

Finally, we reached level ground. My toes ached, and my fingertips felt raw. If not for the germs, I would have kissed the forest floor.

"You did it, Krish. I'm so proud of you."

"That makes two of us."

I followed Dad toward the glimmer of lights at a distance. The forest of bamboo thinned slightly as we approached a clear patch of land.

"Stop!" said a voice from the darkness. "What are you doing here?"

We froze. I looked around but saw no one, though a smell of wet animal hung in the air. Was it the guy who'd told me to run playing games with us again? Despite the exhaustion, I was ready to give him a telling-off if he showed himself. Enough already.

"We're lost," Dad said. "Can you please help us?" I was surprised at how calm and confident he sounded.

A lantern wick glowed bright. My gaze travelled up the hairy hand holding the lantern, to a man's face. It was thin with a long nose and weak chin. His front teeth protruded between gray lips, and his large ears twitched as if listening to something I couldn't hear. It was the red eyes that bothered me the most. Conjunctivitis? I took a step back.

"Namaste," said Dad.

"You should not be here," said the man, sternly.

"You got that right," I said. "This was a *huge* mistake."

Dad dug his fingers into my shoulder. I got the hint.

"My name is Kabir Roy, and this is my son, Krish. As I mentioned before, we got lost during a camping trip. Our GPS isn't working, nor are the radio and cellphone. If you could let us spend the night here and allow us to use your telephone, we'll call for help and be on our way. We would be happy to pay you for boarding and food."

The weird man continued to stare at us. An icy blast swept into the valley. I shivered and sneezed, spraying the villager full on. "Sorry," I said, wiping my sleeve across my nose. "I'm freezing."

Still the man said nothing.

"So, can you provide us shelter for the night?" asked Dad,

his voice tinged with impatience.

"Please," I added. "We're cold and tired and very hungry." I hugged myself tight as the wind sliced through me, causing me to sneeze three times in succession. "And something or someone is following us. Don't send us away." I was willing to beg if need be.

The villager's face softened. "We know what it is to be cold and hungry." He put the lantern on the ground, took off his black fur coat, and draped it over my shoulders. It smelled strange, but was so warm, it felt as if I were slipping into a hot bath. My nose lost the battle against my body as heat spread through me from head to toe.

"Thank you, sir —" I said, pulling the coat tight around me.

"Dorje," he said. "We do not encourage travelers to stop at our village, but it is not safe in the forest. You may stay if you follow our rules. Do you agree?"

I nodded vigorously and looked at Dad.

"Yes, thank you, Dorje," Dad replied.

Dorje turned and hurried on a well-trodden path toward the village. Tonight, we would sleep on a bed, eat hot food, and probably have a chance to bathe.

Felicitations.

We walked across the wide clearing I'd seen while we were descending. Firelight flickered inside the huts and seeped through closed shutters. Close to the ground, shadows moved. The village was infested with rats. I'd educate Dorje first thing tomorrow morning, even though it was these very vermin who'd helped us locate the village.

A thick grove of bamboo, higher than the ones we'd seen in the forest, grew in the middle of the clearing, like an odd centerpiece. A dozen or so villagers sat at a blazing bonfire beside the grove, talking and laughing. Lengths of blackened bamboo smoked inside the fire. I didn't know bamboo was edible. Hopefully that wasn't what they'd offer us for dinner.

As we hurried along, villagers in fur coats similar to the one Dorje had given me walked by, glancing at us. No one stopped us, and I was glad. It took all my willpower to put one foot in front of the other as we followed our guide. I was exhausted and in danger of passing out before we got to a bed.

Dorje stopped in front of a neat A-frame hut some distance away from the clearing. It had a large window with closed shutters. We stepped onto the wide porch and walked through wooden doors. Dorje put the lantern on the floor, and I looked around.

The hut had a packed mud floor that gave off a comforting earthy smell. A single cot, made of bamboo, sat beside the window. A table and two chairs, also of bamboo, were beside the door. A black pot-bellied stove sat in the middle of the room. It was evident that this was the source of heat, and the most important feature, so everything else was arranged around it. There was only one other door leading to the back. There was no indoor bathroom.

"This is the guest house," said Dorje. "Stay. I will bring food and an extra cot."

Before I could ask him about the bathroom, he was already out the door.

As soon as he left, I collapsed on the cot. Though it was chilly, this was so much better than being out in the wind. I shrugged off my backpack. Something poked my side. I remembered the crunch when I'd slipped. Did I dare look down? Would it be a broken body part that hadn't started hurting yet?

It was the radio. Its antenna hung at an odd angle.

Fiddlesticks!

I was glad I had no broken bones, but the radio might have been our only way to call for help if the village didn't have a land line or cellphones! Why hadn't I given it back to Dad instead of keeping it with me?

My stomach cramped with panic, and I had to take deep breaths to calm down.

"We'll fix the radio tomorrow," Dad said, watching me. "I'm sure they'll have spare parts. Don't worry, Krish."

Dad slid his backpack off his shoulders and put it on the floor. "At least we'll be comfortable tonight."

"Tomorrow we get our bearings and head back to camp, even if the radio isn't working," I said. "Right?"

"I wanted to talk to you about that, Krish. I'd like some pictures of this village. It's remote and might be interesting. What say we hang around here for a day or two?"

I stared at my trembling hands, breathing deeply. Why couldn't he see that I was miserable? Or was it that he didn't want to see?

"What is the name of this village?" I asked. "I don't remember seeing one marked on the map."

Dad pulled out the map from his pocket and spread it on the floor. I knelt beside him and smoothed the corners as buttery light from the lantern spilled over it. Dad traced a finger over the route we had taken north from Leh through the Ladakh Range.

"The Adventure Camp is here," he said. "At 34.15 degrees north and 77.57 degrees east. We walked an average of six kilometers an hour, so we should be here: approximately 36 north and 78 east. This is where the village is." His finger stabbed a spot on the map.

"There's nothing marked here but forest," I said, frowning.

Dad looked up at me, his eyes sparkling. "Exactly! Do you

realize the opportunity we have? This is a photographer's dream!"

And his son's nightmare.

The door creaked open, and Dorje appeared with a girl who looked to be about my age. The girl carried a tray, and Dorje brought a burning log in a pail. She nodded at us and set the tray down on the table while Dorje headed for the stove.

"This is Tashi," said Dorje, starting to light a fire. He added logs from a pile by the door. "Our shaman's daughter."

"Hello," I said, unable to stop staring. A large red birthmark covered a side of Tashi's face, vivid against her white skin and silver hair. Her eyes, a light gray, looked cold. She made me uneasy.

Tashi arranged two pieces of charred bamboo, about ten inches in length, and two cups of steaming liquid on the table, and glanced at me. "Obviously you haven't met too many albinos," she said.

I blushed, looking away immediately. She was right: I'd never met an albino. But I should have known better than to stare at her. "Sorry," I mumbled.

"I forgive you," she said, lifting her chin slightly. "We're rare and quite special."

In that very instant, I liked her. She was different, and she owned it.

"I guess you don't like travelers in your village, right?" I said.

"Only if they —" Tashi started to say.

A volley of sharp clicks spilled from Dorje's mouth. Tashi shut up instantly. He'd said something in that click tongue so we wouldn't understand. Dad and I stared at him, hoping he would explain or translate. He didn't. An awkward minute crawled by. Tashi held my gaze silently. I got the feeling she wanted to say something, but not in front of Dorje. I was terrible at physical activities but great at reading silences and looks. This one spoke volumes.

"What *is* this village, Dorje?" asked Dad, peering at the map spread out on the floor.

Good job changing the subject, Dad.

"Imdur," Dorje replied, shutting the stove door with a clang. Sparks leaped through the grate as the logs caught fire and blazed. The smell of woodsmoke filled the room.

"Why can't I find it?" said Dad, his grimy finger still on the map.

Dorje's eyes bored into us; they were like black mirrors reflecting twin flames. "Because we don't want to be found."

CHAPTER 3

The crackling firewood filled the silence. Heat seeped from the pot-bellied stove, and the room warmed up. Dorje and Tashi exchanged a glance. I looked over at Dad, but he was still staring at Dorje.

"Why don't you want anyone to find Imdur?" Dad asked. "I'm curious."

His voice shook ever so slightly. My GF tingled as I realized where he was going with this. Photo op. Fame. Glory. Money. It would be hard tearing him away from here.

Had this been the plan all along? No, Dad wouldn't do that to me. This was a trip for us. Not an assignment. I was tired, and my GF was working overtime.

"Eat your dinner and leave everything outside the door," said Tashi, when Dorje did not reply. "Someone will pick it up later."

"We don't eat bamboo," I said politely. "Though it smells good. Anything else on the menu?"

Tashi gave me a pitying look and reached for one of the bamboo sticks on the table. She popped open a fitted lid with a sharp fingernail. Steam billowed from the hollowed inside, brimming with food. "Chicken and spinach rice," she said. "Think you can eat this?"

"You use hollowed bamboo as cooking pots," I said, hurrying up to the table. "A clean and green solution. Neat!" I smiled at her. "And yes, it smells delicious."

For a second, Tashi's serious expression melted. She returned my smile, which made her look pretty. It faded away immediately. Something was troubling her, and I wanted to help, if I could.

"Sleep well," said Dorje, bowing and making his way to the door.

Tashi slipped out without another word. I decided to keep an eye on her for the short while we were here. Something about her intrigued me.

Dorje had just followed Tashi out the door when I remembered the most important thing. "Just a sec," I called out. "Could you show us the, um ... shower and toilet before you go?" I hoped they would have decent plumbing and running hot water close by. This hut definitely didn't have it.

Tashi left while Dorje led us through the back door and pointed to the outdoor toilet — a hole in the ground (I peeked in) surrounded by a bamboo hut through which the wind whistled a merry tune. Wash-up station was a bucket of water. A thin film of ice glistened in the moonlight, and a plastic mug hung off its side, also encrusted with ice.

Fanfaronade.

"Tomorrow I will show you nature's shower," said Dorje. "You will enjoy it, and it's very good for you." His tone sounded a bit smug.

"Thank you," said Dad, once we were back inside.

"Would you like your coat back?" I asked Dorje, making no move to take it off.

Dorje looked at me gravely. Did the villagers of Imdur have to pay a hefty fine if they smiled? "You can return it when you leave."

"Thanks," I replied. "We'll be off tomorrow, and I'll be sure to find you before we go." It would have been rude to mention that the coat stank.

"I will return with an extra cot," he said and left, shutting the door behind him.

I dug into my backpack, retrieved the bottle of sanitizer, and squirted some on my hands. "Want some?" I asked Dad, holding out the bottle.

"What doesn't kill you makes you stronger," Dad said, grabbing a spoon carved out of bamboo with grimy fingers.

"That's a cliché and a myth. E. coli is very debilitating, and it takes days to recover."

"Agree to disagree?" said Dad, smiling. He was in a great mood, and we both knew why.

I reached for a spoon beside the charred bamboo and dug in. I was starving, and the food was delicious. The flavor of chicken with ginger, garlic, and spices exploded in my mouth as I devoured it. The steaming liquid turned out to be buttery tea, which slid down my throat, warming my insides. I'd never had tea with butter in it, but Dad explained that it was quite common to have tea this way, especially for people in North India and Tibet.

After eating rehydrated food since we left camp, this was a feast. I couldn't help but remember the last meal I'd enjoyed so much — Mom's baked lasagna. Suddenly, I missed her, and the next bite was harder to get past the lump in my throat.

"I want to go home, Dad. I've had enough of this. I know — I *know* this was my idea," I said, cutting him off when he opened his mouth to speak, "but this is a lot harder than I thought it would be. I can't do it. I don't want to."

Dad took another mouthful and chewed. He swallowed and looked at me. "This is the opportunity of a lifetime, Krish. If we leave now, I may not be able to come back. Can you not bear with me for a few days while I take pictures? You'll be doing me a huge favor. Who knows, you might even get to like this place. Tashi seems like a nice kid. Maybe you can make friends and find out some more about Imdur for the article to accompany my pictures."

I hated this place — the cold, dirt, and germs. I was sure this village was overrun with rats, even though the inhabitants seemed okay. But I'd disappointed Dad so often, this could be my chance to make it up to him. I wanted him to look at me the same way he looked at my cousin Anjali. I *needed* him to be proud of me. And yet, the rats made my skin crawl. It was my turn to take a bite of food and chew slowly as I considered his request.

I glanced around the guest house. It was warm, relatively clean, and dry. Better than camping in the forest in the bitter cold. I could give him two days. Maybe that would change his opinion of me. I might not be a good camper, but I could manage to live in the village even though it was a back-to-nature scenario.

"Two days," I said, watching his face. "Then we're out of here."

Dad's mouth drooped as he took another bite, staring at the glowing stove. It felt like someone had kicked me in the chest. Did he even realize how much it cost me to agree to *two days*? I didn't know which one of us was more disappointed.

"Okay, Krish, two days it is, and thank you," he said finally. "I know this is hard for you, and it means a lot to me."

It was a small gesture, and yet, I knew he was disappointed.

Something told me that even now he was comparing me to Anjali, who would've been happy to stay here as long as Dad wanted. I was fighting a losing battle, and a part of me wanted to give up, have a meltdown, go home. I quieted the voice and managed a tiny smile.

Dad shovelled another spoonful of food into his mouth. "If I sell this to *National Geographic*, I'll be famous — and you'll have a byline on this photo story, for sure."

"I'll ask Dorje for spare parts for the radio tomorrow," I replied, trying not to let the doubts show on my face.

"We'll also ask if there's a telephone in the village or if any of them possess a cellphone," said Dad. "We'll get word to the camp and tell them to pick us up in two days. This'll be fun. I appreciate you being so brave about it, Krish. Truly."

I wanted Dad to get his pictures. They meant a lot to him and made him happy. Almost as much as Anjali's friendship had meant to me, at one time. I pushed the thought away. No point distracting myself now, thinking about that terrible summer when things changed between us forever. My cousin and best friend had become a polite stranger.

Dorje returned, dragging a second bamboo cot and bedding. We both jumped up to help him, but he waved us away. "Sit. I can manage."

Other than the fact that Dorje talked to us as if we were

pets or idiots, he didn't seem too bad. He'd given me his coat and allowed us to stay, even if his social skills needed a bit of polish.

Quickly, efficiently, he maneuvered the cots on either side of the stove. We would be warm and dry tonight. Now if only there'd been a hot shower, life would have been sweet. But this was a huge improvement on the last twenty-four hours, and I refused to dwell on things I couldn't have right now. I tossed back the last of the tea, ready to jump into bed.

Dorje laid out thin mattresses on the bamboo frames, covered them with clean cotton sheets, and threw on patchwork quilts and a couple of pillows. As soon as he was done, he hurried to the door. Sounds of revelry wafted in, along with the smell of wet fur and spices. He looked at us sternly, and once again I felt like a child or a puppy.

"Do not leave the guest house at night. No matter what you hear, stay inside. Understand?"

"Why?" said Dad.

"What's out there?" I added, sweat gathering in my pits.

"Wild animals," he said in a dramatic whisper. "It's not safe."

I remembered the mystery shadow. "What's really in the forest, Dorje? I thought I saw something or someone following us. It was a person, not an animal, I'm sure of that."

Dad laughed. "My son has an active imagination."

"Not this time," said Dorje. His eyes darted between us, and his voice dropped to a whisper. "These forests are ancient and full of evil spirits: ghosts who refuse to leave us. They kill people. Safest to stay indoors at night."

Now that was taking things a bit too far. Did we have *IDIOT* printed on our foreheads?

Dad smiled politely. I gave Dorje a stony look. "What about the bathroom? Can I go outside if I have to use it?" I had a habit of getting up several times a night to pee. Especially when stressed or in unfamiliar surroundings. Tonight, it was a cert.

"You can use the toilet in the courtyard at the back, but do not wander into the village. Those are our rules, and you have agreed to follow them."

I was starting to feel drowsy. I wasn't stepping out of the guest house, to the courtyard or the village, once I was under the covers. Dad might, not me.

"Sure," Dad said. The look in his eyes belied his words.

"Breakfast will be served near the bamboo grove in the center of the village. Everyone meets there, and we eat together. Join us whenever you wake up."

"Thank you, we will," said Dad.

I nodded.

"Good night," said Dorje and shut the door.

"You're not planning on sneaking out, Dad, are you?"

Dad shook his head and yawned. "Not tonight. I'm too tired. But tomorrow night, for sure. This place is fascinating."

Dad was a kid in a candy shop. He had his camera and the chance to photograph an off-the-map village. I'd agreed to let him have two days without whining. Life was as good as it was going to get.

I forced myself to use the outdoor toilet before I hit the bed. It was weird "going" while a cold wind whistled through the cracks in the bamboo outhouse. I scooped out icy water from the bucket and washed up. Once again, I got the feeling someone was watching my every move. Not rats — something else.

Hands numb, teeth chattering like a toy monkey's, I raced inside. I wasn't drinking any more water till tomorrow morning. I couldn't face another trip outside in this brutal cold. Dad had already gathered the dinner things and put them on the doorstep out front.

"Something strange is going on in the village," said Dad, peering through a crack in the shutters. "There's activity near the bamboo grove, but because we're so far back, I can't get a clear shot, even with my telephoto lens. I think they deliberately put us here so we can't see anything. Maybe I should step outside for a quick look."

"You promised you wouldn't go out tonight." I couldn't

stand it if the villagers caught him and threw us both out tonight. Even if we got through to Adventure Camp, we'd have at least a day's wait in the forest till we were rescued. It was safer to wait here, in relative comfort and cleanliness.

"Always the rule-follower." Dad sounded annoyed. "Try to be a little adventurous, Krish, and a bit curious."

Too tired to argue, I climbed into bed. The bamboo creaked. I slung the coat at the foot of the bed and slid under the cotton quilt. It smelled of sunshine with an underlying whiff of wet fur, which I had now come to expect. But it was warm and dry. Heaven.

"Night, Dad."

After a long minute, he replied. "Night, Krish."

I WOKE UP SUDDENLY to the sound of someone singing in a language I didn't understand. The voice rose and fell in a lament. My chest ached with sadness. The song died away and was replaced by the murmur of voices.

Glancing at my watch, I realized it was 3:00 a.m. The village was still awake? These guys were party animals and would feel right at home in the city.

There was a repeated *thwack* — as if someone were chopping wood. Voices were swept away by the whisper of wind through the bamboo. The flames in the stove leaped up, and I snuggled deeper under the covers.

I heard scrabbling near the back door. Rats!

The sounds shifted from the back to the front of the house. It was just outside the window now, as if rats were digging, trying to get in. The mud floor and bamboo walls wouldn't keep them out for long.

I jumped out of bed, shivering, and grabbed Dorje's coat. Instant warmth. Fumbling with the latch on the window, I opened it a tiny crack. Cold air rushed in. Dad continued to sleep.

Easing open the window, I tried to get a glimpse of what was going on in the village. As I stuck my head out the window to get a good look, someone darted around the side. He or she had the same height and build as the shadow I'd seen in the forest. My GF tingled. Had that mystery person followed us here? Should I wake Dad? He was sure to get annoyed with me for waking him because of a shadow.

In a horror movie, this would be the part when Idiot Character would go out to investigate, flashlight in hand, eerie music thumping in the background. Idiot Character would get mauled or killed. I had *zero* intention of wandering out in the dark to investigate a mystery shadow. I would ask Dorje about it in the morning.

I tiptoed back to the bed, thankful that I didn't have to pee. But the second I thought of it, I had to go. I willed my brain to ignore my bladder. No use.

"Dad!" I whispered. "I have to go. Don't you?"

"No," he said, and went back to sleep.

Febricity!

I was sure there'd be a mini zoo running around in the outdoor toilet at this time of night. If rats, lizards, and cockroaches could inhabit a public toilet in Delhi, this one was sure to have a larger menagerie. Might even have a poisonous snake or two, waiting to bite my bum.

Stop it, Krish.

I slipped on my boots, padded to the back door, and stepped out, flashlight at the ready. Cold air blasted my face. My breath fogged as I gave the courtyard a once-over with the flashlight. Nothing moved.

I reminded myself that the villagers were awake, so if I screamed for help, someone would hear me. I would go quickly and be back in under a minute. No problem at all. None.

I ran to the outhouse and opened the door. A stink wafted out. I did my business quickly. It felt *so* good to let go. Bladder empty, I hurried back and stopped short. A white blob on the ground glowed in the moonlight. It was a large white rat, its pink tail twice as long as its body. It stood on its hind legs, between me and the back door, watching. It looked like the one that had bitten my bum, but larger.

"Shoo!" I said, stamping the ground. My skin crawled as

I realized the back door was still open. What if it ran into the hut instead of away? How could I have forgotten to close the door? Thoughts of the rat biting me while I slept flashed through my head. Infection, inflammation, painful death.

"SHOO!" I said again, a little louder.

The rat cleaned its whiskers and continued staring at me. City rats would have bolted at the sight of humans. This one was cheeky and needed to be taught a lesson.

That's right, Krish. Show it who's boss.

I took a step back, keeping an eye on the rat. A large stone was within reach.

"Last chance," I said, advancing. "Either you run or I'll smash you to a pulp."

The rat squeaked. Was it taunting me?

I was about to hurl the stone when someone grabbed my hand in a steely grip. I screamed and pulled it away, whirling around.

Dorje's eyes were blazing. "NO!"

"What is wrong with you?" I yelled. "Rats are carriers of deadly diseases. Just look at it!"

I swung the flashlight back. *Whoa!* Dad stood there, and the rat had disappeared.

"Did you see it, Dad? The white rat? Did it run inside? We have to find it —"

"Stop blabbering, Krish," Dad said, rubbing the sleep out of his eyes. "What's all this racket in the middle of the night?"

That hurt. Why did he have to snap at me in front of Dorje? "I went out to pee and saw a huge white rat. I thought it might run into our hut and tried to kill it. Dorje stopped me."

Dad looked around. "Where is it?"

"Gone." I turned to Dorje. "We've got to find it now."

"No!" Dorje repeated. "Rats are God's creatures, and we, the Imdura, do *not* harm them. You agreed to follow our rules. You are breaking your word."

"Sorry, Dorje," Dad said. "My son is a germophobe and thinks every little rodent is a death threat. We'll follow your rules. Come *on*, Krish, back to bed."

"No! I heard scrabbling. These rats were trying to get into the guest house, and I'm not waiting for one to bite me while I sleep."

"If you touch a single rat, you will be thrown out of the village right now," said Dorje. He drew himself up and hissed at us. His nose quivered, and his eyes blazed.

Dad strode over and yanked me so hard he almost pulled my arm out of the socket. I winced. "That is enough —" Dad started to say.

"Yes, that is enough," a gentle voice cut in.

We both turned to face the shadows beside the hut. A

woman with silver hair and a long white robe walked toward us. The only color on her was a large red bindi in the middle of her forehead. Dorje bowed his head and pressed his hands together in a namaste.

"Imma," he whispered. "I had this under control."

The woman came up to us. She removed Dad's hand from my arm and stroked my cheek. Her light gray eyes gazed into mine, and I felt a calm I hadn't experienced in a long while.

"Violence is never the answer to any problem," she said, frowning at Dad. "This child needs to understand what he is doing wrong before you punish him."

Dad looked mutinous. "Who are *you* to tell me how to behave with my son?"

"I am the shaman of this village," she replied, staring at him. "Everyone calls me Imma."

Dad's eyes widened. "I'm sorry," he said in a friendlier voice. "We won't touch any rats. Right, Krish?"

So, this was Tashi's mom. I looked into Imma's serene face. I had to speak up, and I knew, somehow, she wouldn't mind the truth. "But, Imma, rats and humans cannot live together. They have to be destroyed because they carry diseases."

She chuckled as if I'd said something funny. "Why don't we continue this discussion in the morning? For now, let us all get some rest."

I nodded. My teeth were chattering despite the coat. Dad hurried inside. I followed, reluctantly.

"Are you deliberately trying to get us thrown out of Imdur, Krish?" Dad said once we'd shut the door. "Is this your way of worming out of the deal we made? That's not fair. I am very disappointed in you."

"I didn't want the rat inside the hut. That's all." I was tired of this constant reminder that I was not living up to his expectations. I wanted to yell back, *Stop already, I'm trying my best.*

"It's not like we're buying a home here," Dad said, pacing the tiny room. "Just follow the rules long enough to let me get decent pictures, and then we'll leave. Can you please do that for me, or is it too much to ask?"

"Why did you have to tell Dorje that I was a germophobe?" I tried to keep my voice steady. Soon the whole village would know, including Tashi. Somehow, that made me feel worse.

Dad sat beside me. "I'm sorry — you're right. I shouldn't have mentioned it, but I was worried when you screamed. It turned out to be nothing at all."

"A filthy rat is not nothing."

Dad sighed. "We've eaten dinner prepared by the Imdura. We're okay, aren't we?"

I nodded.

"So, all good? We still have two days, and you'll get acclimated in no time. Mark my words."

I popped a candy into my mouth and held it under my tongue. The sweetness reduced my anxiety. Two more days and a night to go. How would I get through them?

As I was falling asleep, I suddenly remembered something. What had Dorje been doing outside our hut in the middle of the night? Had he been the shadow lurking around, here and in the forest?

Imdur was weird, and so were its inhabitants. Except Imma. I liked her.

CHAPTER 4

A patch on my forehead glowed warm, and I opened my eyes. A beam of sunlight pointed at me from a crack in the window. After the run-in with the rat, I'd slept peacefully the remainder of the night. I felt rested and very hungry.

"Morning, Dad," I said, sitting up.

He was gone. His camera case lay on the bed, empty. Dad wasn't wasting a single minute. Good! The sooner he got his pictures, the sooner we could leave.

I lay in bed a few minutes longer, reluctant to leave the warm cocoon. My sketchbook and colored pencils were in my backpack, within easy reach. I did a quick sketch of the guest house, and before I realized it, I'd sketched Tashi — her silvery hair, intense gray eyes, and birthmark. I shut the sketchbook, slipped it into its protective plastic cover, and pushed it deep into the backpack under my clothes. Besides candies, sketching was the only thing that helped me relax.

The outdoor bathroom was freezing. My breath fogged, and goosebumps covered every inch of exposed skin. The water in the bucket had a thin layer of ice again. I bashed it with the mug, scooped up the frigid water, and tried to wash up without screaming. Someone had left a rough bar of soap beside the bucket. It smelled of bamboo, and I used it liberally, feeling slightly cleaner after I was done. I'd have traded a candy and my little toe for a hot shower.

Back in the guest house, I switched on the satellite radio. Not a peep even with fresh batteries. I clipped it on to my belt. If Dorje found me a spare part, I was sure I could fix it. There was plenty of duct tape in my backpack — a must-have on a camping trip, per the outdoor survival video I'd watched quite a few times.

I took a quick inventory of my stash of candies. I'd eaten one in the forest after the scare with the mysterious person, and one more last night. There were nine left. I'd have to ration them to help me get through the next two days.

Slipping on Dorje's coat, I stepped out of the hut and inhaled crisp, cold air. The mountains seemed close enough to touch. My gaze travelled up the lush green slopes, covered mostly with bamboo. It was starting to flower, and the air smelled sweet.

The highest peaks were white, as if covered with melting scoops of vanilla ice cream. A stark reminder that winter was almost upon us. The Adventure Camp counsellors had said that in a month, the snowfall would be so heavy that the mountains would be impassable.

THE IMDURA HAD BUILT their huts in widening rings around the bamboo grove, like ripples on a pond. Though I'd caught a glimpse of it during the descent, I could see it more clearly now. Though it was mid-morning, the village was strangely quiet. As I meandered through the bamboo huts toward the grove in the center, I wondered why the Imdura were goofing off when they should be working. Why party all night when they should be sleeping? Also, why were they obsessed with rats? This was a weird place, and I couldn't wait to leave.

I kept a lookout for Dad and Imma. The way she'd made Dad calm down without raising her voice had been awesome. But there was no sign of them, or anyone else. The village seemed deserted. My footsteps crunching on the ground, interspersed with occasional squeaks, were the only sounds.

A hut with a bright red door, larger and more intricately carved than any other in the village, caught my eye. A clay plate sat in the center of a bright chalk pattern on this and every porch. I made a mental note to ask someone about their significance.

Just then the red door opened, and Tashi walked out. She wore a long-sleeved white tunic, white pants, and an ankle-length fur coat like mine. A knitted hat in red, orange, and green perched jauntily on her head. "Did you sleep well?" she said softly. "I was just coming to get you."

"Saved you the trouble," I said with a smile. I'd liked her ever since she'd put me in my place for staring. I could learn a thing or two from her about confidence.

She nodded without smiling.

"Why are you always so serious?" I asked. "Is laughing a crime in Imdur?"

"I am the next shaman," she said. "I have to be dignified at all times."

"So, no smiling, no jokes, and absolutely no fun at all," I said. "Got it."

Her lips twitched. She was cool, in a weird way.

"Time for breakfast," she said and started walking. I fell into step beside her.

Multicoloured flags hanging around the perimeter of the village snapped in the stiff breeze. All the huts were in good shape despite the battering they must take each winter. The wooden doors were carved with intricate patterns, and the window shutters were painted in reds, blues, and yellows. My fingers itched for my coloured pencils and sketchbook.

As we walked in a comfortable silence, the sunlight caught the silky fur of our coats. They glistened, reminding me of the bear that used to dance in the streets of Delhi. I had loved watching it when I was young. As I grew older and read about the torture animals go through in captivity, though, I hated even the mention of the zoo, let alone a visit to it.

"What animal is this coat made of?" I asked, almost afraid to know the answer. "It's very warm." If it involved torture, I'd have to take it off immediately, and I didn't want to. I had to know the truth, though.

"Guess," said Tashi, not meeting my eyes.

"Black bear?"

"No."

"Panther?"

"No."

I didn't notice where I was stepping, and something under my boot squeaked. I almost fell over. As a black rat shot away, I made the connection.

"Careful!" she snapped. "You almost stepped on my —"

"Rats?" I whispered, cutting her off. I wasn't sure if I was more horrified that it was rat fur or that she'd almost admitted it was her pet. Why else would she say *my*?

Tashi nodded.

I ripped the coat off and hurled it away. Bile rose in my throat. I'd been caressing and snuggling into rat fur since we'd stepped into the village. I'd even slept with it!

"Dorje stopped me from killing a rat last night. To make a coat you need to skin them. And to make a coat of this length, you must have slaughtered hundreds. You're all hypocrites."

Tashi's face was serene. "These rats died of natural causes. Before burying them, we skinned them. This way, we are always close to our ancestors. We look after them while they live, and they look after us when they're dead. It is a complete cycle — don't you see the beauty of it?"

I made another connection as I glanced at the plates of white paste on every porch. "This is food to feed the rats?" I said, pointing.

"Yes," said Tashi. "We feed them the very best rice paste in butter. They love it."

In every other part of the world, including Delhi, we'd be setting rat traps. I shivered with cold and horror as it dawned on me: Imdur must be exploding with rats. They multiplied quickly and had large litters. This little bit of trivia didn't help, but my mind was not selective in the type or timeliness of information it provided.

Tashi retrieved the coat and held it out to me. "You will

need it when it's so cold, you can't feel your fingers or toes. Imagine it to be any fur, but please don't throw it away or give it back to Dorje."

Though my panic was ballooning, I knew what she said was true. In two days, we'd be out of here. Why freeze till then? Even though I felt squeamish, my hands moved automatically, slipping the coat on. It felt like stepping into the summer sun from a long, dark tunnel.

Tashi smiled. It was much better than her frown-face. "You are being smart and practical. I like that."

We arrived at the grove. A few villagers were milling around. Dad, with his camera slung on his shoulder, was talking animatedly with two men beside the fire. He ate with gusto, scooping up food from a wooden bowl. The Imdura were nodding. I was still squeamish about the coat, but it was keeping me warm. I decided not to think about it anymore.

"Let's get some food," said Tashi, glancing at me shrewdly. "I will be your guide till you leave."

"We don't need one," I said. I got the feeling she could read my mind, and I didn't want to be stuck with her all day, observing me.

"Imma has said you do, and she is the final word in this village," Tashi replied. She didn't look happy, and I wondered if Imma had forced her. And more importantly, why?

"Where can I find her?" I asked. "I have a few things to discuss."

"She will find you when she is ready," said Tashi.

The bamboo was twice as tall as Dad. Thick green leaves sprouted along its length. Parts of it were scratched and gouged. No matter where I turned, I was reminded of the rats.

A villager squatted beside the cooking fire, in which steamed a dozen lengths of charred bamboo. A young boy with sharp features fetched more wood from a pile of logs a short distance away. Porridge bubbled in some of the bamboo sections, while others had a thick yellow custard that I assumed was egg.

The villagers shovelled food into their mouths hurriedly. Young and old, they were variations of Dorje: thin faces with lean, muscular bodies. Their eyes constantly darted around. What kind of danger made them so twitchy and alert?

"Ahh, Krish, you're awake," said Dad. "Sleep well?"

"Yes, Dad. I see you got an early start." I glanced at the camera.

"Busy day," he said and winked. "I'm on a tight schedule, didn't you know?"

He was keeping his word and seemed to be in a good mood. We had to get the radio working first, though. It was my top priority.

An old guy was seated so close to the fire, if he toppled in, he'd go up in flames. Gnarled hands with pointed yellow nails were curved around his wooden bowl. His cloudy eyes stared into mine with suspicion and hostility. I wished I could tell him that I didn't want to be here just as much as he didn't want me to be here. My GF advised me to zip it.

He spoke in a thin, quavering voice. "Tashi, introduce me to this young man."

"Yes, Great-Grandfather," said Tashi and led me forward. "This is Krish. He and his father were lost in the forest. They found us last night and asked to stay. Krish, this is my great-grandfather, Shalva, the oldest person in Imdur."

I joined my hands in a namaste, unable to stop staring. His face had more lines than a topographic world map. Matted gray hair covered his head, and a row of red-stained teeth peeked out between chapped lips. Yikes, didn't he use a toothbrush at all?

Shalva returned my namaste with shaky hands. "Get him some breakfast," he said.

"I'll help!" This from the boy with the sharp features and shifty look.

"That's my brother, Norbu, who's a pest," said Tashi, grimacing.

Thin, wiry, and extremely twitchy, Norbu made me nervous just by looking at him.

"You are worse," said Norbu as he waited for a villager to fill up a bowl with food. He presented it to me, watching closely. The porridge was gooey and gray. Beside it was a mound of yellow curds flecked with green.

"Thanks," I said, wondering if this might be my last meal, given the number of rats around here. But I'd survived dinner. Hopefully, I would survive breakfast too.

Norbu stuck his tongue out at Tashi and scampered off.

I sniffed the bowl. It smelled sweet and savoury.

"Cracked wheat with jaggery and scrambled eggs with spring onions," said Dad, noticing my hesitation. He scraped the bottom of the bowl and put the last spoonful into his mouth. "It's delicious. Try it, Krish."

I scooped up a tiny spoonful, aware that everyone was watching me. To reject food was to reject the Imdura and their hospitality. *Please don't taste gross.* My hand shook, and I hoped they wouldn't notice. The porridge tasted almost like oatmeal. I liked it. I took a bite of egg. Very good. I gave the cook a thumbs-up and devoured the rest.

Dad looked relieved. Tashi studied me with a thoughtful expression. She was perceptive and somehow knew I'd been worried about the food. But if she'd had doubts, she hadn't ratted me out. We might even be good friends by the time I left. I missed having someone to talk to now that Anjali and I were no longer best buds. Neither her father (Dad's brother), Naveen Uncle, nor Dad knew about our fight. By unspoken agreement, we'd kept it a secret.

"Thank you for an excellent breakfast," said Dad, handing his bowl back. "We would appreciate a tour of the village. Or we could just wander around on our own."

I stared at Dad. "Don't we have to get the radio working first so we can contact Adventure Camp to pick us up? I'm sure Naveen Uncle and Anjali must be worried about us."

"I've asked Dorje already, and he said he'll look for a spare antenna," Dad said, frowning at me. "He's offered to repair it for us, so hand it over when you see him."

"I'm sure Dorje has plenty to do," I said. "I'll do it myself, if I can get a spare part." I was aware that Shalva and the villagers were following our exchange closely. "Is there a telephone in the village, or can we borrow someone's cellphone?"

"No," Shalva replied. "We have no need for useless things that disturb our peace. Besides, we are too remote for a phone line or a cell tower."

Wow. The Imdura took staying under the radar pretty seriously.

"Fair enough," said Dad, sidling away from the fire. "That's it, then. We'll wander around on our own. No need to trouble anyone." He looked eager to get started photographing the village.

"Guests are the avatars of God," said Shalva. "If you wish to see Imdur, Tashi and Dorje will show you around." His breath smelled of egg and raw meat. I moved upwind.

"Surely we don't need two guides," said Dad, his fingers fiddling with the dials on his camera. "One will suffice. None is even better."

"I insist, for your own safety," said Shalva. "Tashi, get Dorje and show our guests around the village. Don't go too far."

Tashi hurried away. Was our safety important, or was this guide business an excuse to keep an eye on us? GF promptly informed me it was the latter.

"One more thing," said Shalva, pointing a shaky finger at Dad's camera. "No pictures."

Dad could not have looked more crushed if he'd been buried in an avalanche. "What?" he spluttered. "Why?"

"We like our peace and quiet," said Shalva. "Pictures mean publicity, and we do not want people here."

"Surely a few pictures of the valley can't hurt?" Dad's face was flushed, and his hands made bumps in his pockets, as if he'd clenched them into fists.

Shalva glared at Dad. "It is *our* duty to look after our guests. It is *your* duty to follow the wishes of your hosts. No pictures."

Dad's eyes turned hard, and I knew that look very well. Telling him not to use the camera was like telling him to hold his breath. He was going to take pictures anyway.

But if he got caught? Nothing would be more embarrassing than being scolded for something we were warned not to do.

"What kind of wild animals live around here?" I asked, when the silence stretched painfully. "We saw something odd last night."

The villagers looked at Shalva. He shook his head imperceptibly. They were hiding something. A hidden village with a secret. If I were the adventurous type, I'd have wanted to solve the mystery, but honestly, I just wanted to go home. I'd had enough of the outdoors to last me for this lifetime and the next.

"The usual," he said. "Monkeys, leopards, deer."

Liars. Why couldn't they just give us a straight answer or say nothing?

Dad refused to meet my eyes. He fidgeted, waiting for Tashi to return with Dorje. Something about the Imdura made me uneasy. Why couldn't Dad feel it too? If it had been up to me, I would have voted to skip the pictures and get as far away from here as possible. But Dad would never give up an opportunity like this, and a part of me respected his dedication to his career.

I finished the last of my breakfast and handed the bowl back. A few villagers, who'd already been here when we arrived, moved away, bowing their heads respectfully toward Shalva. I finally got my first glimpse of the bamboo grove, all the way to the ground. A large clay plate filled with porridge and eggs lay at its base.

It swarmed with rats.

CHAPTER 5

Electricity crackled over my skin, and I felt light-headed. Staring at the vermin, I tasted my breakfast a second time. They'd been so quiet, I hadn't realized there were so many, *so close by*. I tried to look away but couldn't. It was as if I were paralyzed.

The rats, having eaten their fill, raced into holes in the ground. More poured out and scurried toward the food in a black stream. Some shinnied up the bamboo poles and disappeared into the foliage, flicking their pink tails. A large, scabby one climbed into Shalva's lap. He stroked it gently, murmuring to it, and it seemed to answer back. What would a rat say — nice gnawing you?

I shuffled backward, desperately in need of a candy. The villagers were treating vermin as pets. No wonder Imdur was overrun. I wanted to disinfect myself, inside and out.

The Imdura had to be educated.

"Let me tell y—" I started to say, but Dad dug his fingers into my shoulder. A villager approached the clearing and went straight to the platter covered with rats. He prayed silently. Then he headed toward the cook, who handed him a bowl of porridge and eggs.

"We'll wait for Dorje in our hut," Dad said to Shalva. "Thank you for breakfast."

I couldn't get myself to thank them for contaminated food. I hurried away, not meeting anyone's eyes, though I felt Shalva's dark gaze following me.

"That's *gross*," I said to Dad when we were out of earshot. "The food we're eating is full of germs. We're going to get sick and die. We have to tell them the truth, or I won't be able to eat another bite as long as we're here."

"Rat worship is not very common in India," said Dad. "The only place I know of is the Karni Mata temple in Rajasthan, which is home to twenty thousand rats. People from all over India come to worship them. It's a major tourist attraction. It seems the Imdura have taken it to the next level. If I could get a picture of *this* village, I'd prove there was another community of rat worshippers." He looked back wistfully at the rats, still scrambling around in the plate, some so bloated they could barely move. I shuddered.

"You're not making this up?"

"Krish, I'm a nature photographer. It is my job to keep an eye out for unusual photo ops, so no, I am *not* making this up. The Karni Mata temple has been photographed too often. *National Geographic* has also done a story on it, so there's no novelty there. But I don't believe anyone has photographed Imdur. *I'd* be the first."

He glanced around. Seeing no one along the pathway to the guest house, he raised his camera. His voice was muffled as he looked through the viewfinder, clicking away. "I was ecstatic when I was asked to find and photograph ..." He stopped, lowered the camera, and gave me a sheepish look.

I felt sick to my stomach, and it had nothing to do with the food or the rats. I stared at Dad, but he didn't meet my eyes, continuing to play with the dials. My GF had been right. This had *never* been about us bonding. This had been an assignment, and it was a timely coincidence that I'd asked to go on a trip. Dad had lied to me.

I hurried toward the guest house on shaky feet, but Dad caught my hand. "I see you've figured it out, Krish, and you're right. This is an assignment, but it was based on rumours, and no one, least of all me, thought there might be any truth to it. We just got lucky, and it was thanks to you, really. I'm sorry I didn't tell you everything, but I knew how worried you were about this trip and didn't want to add to it."

"The lie makes it worse," I said. "What if you had to choose between your assignment and me?" I already knew the answer, but I wanted to hear him say it.

"Come on, Krish," Dad said, taking a deep breath. "You

and your mother mean more to me than anything else in the world." He crouched and put his hands on my shoulders. "You believe me, don't you?"

I looked away, not knowing what to believe. He'd lied to me, then begged for two days here even though he knew I was miserable. Did that not prove the assignment came first?

"No," I said and started to walk away. "Leave me alone and go take your pictures." I couldn't bear to be near him at the moment.

Dad enveloped me in a hug. I fought hard, but he held me tight till I stopped fighting. "Krish, I know how difficult this is for you, and I'm so proud of you for trying. Truly I am. You're doing great so far."

I pulled away and looked him in the eye. "Another lie so I'll agree to stay longer?"

He shook his head. "I mean it."

"When can we leave?"

"As soon as I'm done," Dad said. "I'm going to work hard all day, and we'll be out of here in no time. I promise." His voice dropped to a whisper. "This village is thriving in the most inhospitable environment. They have no modern amenities, no electricity, and yet they're self-sufficient. They're using bamboo, a clean and green solution, in so many ways. There is *so much* we can learn from them, and it is my duty to bring this story to the world."

Before I could reply, there was a cough. We whirled around. Dorje and Tashi stood a short distance away, watching us. They were both carrying spears. I hoped they hadn't heard our conversation, or we'd be in serious trouble. Dad's face was pale. "Wow, you guys sure move quietly. Krish and I didn't hear you arrive at all. All good on this fine day?" He was babbling, and I glanced up at him. He stopped talking.

Dorje and Tashi exchanged a look. Dorje clicked his tongue. Tashi answered back in the same way.

"Why do you have spears?" I asked.

"The forest has wild things," said Dorje when I continued to stare at him. "I already told you that. This is to keep us all safe. Ready?"

"I'm coming too." Norbu came racing toward us.

"No," said Tashi. "You are to stay with Great-Grandfather."

"You're not shaman yet," said Norbu. "I don't take orders from you, only Imma."

"*I'm* in charge right now, and I say you go back," said Dorje, sternly. "Or Imma will hear about this."

Norbu glowered at him and ran off. Dorje took the lead, with Dad behind him. Tashi was next, and I followed last.

"Hand over your camera, please," said Dorje as we walked. "Taking pictures is strictly forbidden, as Shalva has already told you. I will give it back when you leave Imdur."

"Why?" Dad sounded as if he were in pain. "I won't take any pictures of the village, but what's wrong with photographing the mountains, the valley? Surely those don't belong to you."

Part of me was happy to hear him this upset. Now he would realize what it felt like to want something badly and not get it, just the way I wanted to go home but had to wait two days so he could photograph this ghastly place.

"Because we are a quiet village," said Dorje. "And we want to stay off the map."

Dad muttered under his breath as he handed his precious camera over to Dorje. It looked as if he were handing over a kidney. Suddenly, I was ashamed of myself for wanting him to suffer when he was only trying to do his job while helping me conquer my phobias. This was not the first time he'd tried, and I had to appreciate his perseverance.

"I'll catch up," said Dad, stopping to tie his shoelace.

Dorje nodded and walked on with Tashi by his side.

"I'll make some sketches when we get back," I whispered to Dad when Dorje and Tashi were out of earshot. "You'll have some kind of record even if you can't take pictures."

"Thanks, Krish," he said and squeezed my hand.

In that moment, if felt like we had a connection, no matter how fragile.

"Faster," said Dorje, glancing back at us. "We don't have all day."

"*We* do," said Dad. "You're free to carry on with your tasks. We'll look around on our own."

Dorje ignored him, as I knew he would.

The climb became steeper. Tashi and Dorje didn't break a sweat. Dad walked easily too. It felt as if someone had tied weights to my ankles, and I gasped for breath, making a mental note to start working out as soon as I got back home. I was hopelessly out of shape.

The stink of something rotting filled the air. I covered my mouth and nose with the upturned collar of my jacket, taking shallow breaths. Would I survive this trip? Was I going to die here? The thought made me stumble, and Tashi, who'd fallen behind to keep me company, grabbed my hand to steady me.

"Are you okay?" she asked. "You're not going to die on me, right?"

"I'm fine," I said, annoyed that she could see how out of shape I was.

"You hate our village," said Tashi. "In fact, you can't wait to get out. You're only here because your father wants to stay. Right?"

I glanced at her. She didn't look angry, just curious.

"It's very different from Delhi," I said, plodding along,

trying not to pant audibly. "My home is a lot more comfortable, and I'm an indoors kind of guy. No offence."

"You're very honest," she said.

"I'm sorry, Tashi. I didn't mean to insult you or your home."

"Your heart is pure," she said suddenly, giving me a sideways glance. "I can see that clearly. But his isn't." She jerked her chin toward Dad.

I don't know why, but that compliment meant a lot to me, warming up my insides like a bellyful of hot chocolate. I let the one about Dad slide. Right now, I was in no mood to defend him. "Thanks," I said.

"What's Delhi like?" Her expression was wistful. "I've always wondered about life in a city."

"I'll tell you all about it when we get back," I said. "I can show you my sketches, too."

"Yes," she said, smiling. "I'd like that."

"Sure," I said, trying to sound calm, though my pulse galloped.

The sound of racing water filled the silence as I hurried to keep up with Dorje and Dad. Suddenly, my stomach roiled. Nothing seemed out of place, and yet my GF was on high alert. Something bad was about to happen.

I grabbed Tashi and pulled her back just as a large boulder landed on the spot where she'd been standing. Tashi screamed and fell backwards, dropping the spear.

Dorje ran back, cursing. I saw a blur in the bushes and then silence. I remembered the shadow I'd seen the previous evening. Was someone trying to kill Tashi? Or was that stone for me? Was it the same person who'd told me to run when we'd been lost?

"Are you okay?" I asked, barely able to stand on my wobbling legs.

Tashi's face was so white, she was almost transparent. She stood up, brushed mud from her clothes, and retrieved her spear. "You saved my life. Thank you."

"It was a gut feel," I said, glancing at Dad. "Most people think it's an overactive imagination. Luckily, I don't."

Dad said nothing as he peered into the bushes and then at Dorje, waiting for him to make the next move.

"Thank you, Krish," said Dorje, glaring at Tashi. He marched toward the bushes and squatted, uttering sharp clicks and chitters.

Goosebumps rose on the back of my neck as the ground trembled slightly under my feet. The bushes rustled, and the air filled with squeaks that grew fainter and then were gone. A stink of ammonia lingered in the air.

"What was that?" I said, staring at Dorje and Tashi. I'd heard them talk "click," but had he just communicated with the rats and told them what to do? I glanced at Dad, and he shook his head.

"Let's go," said Dorje, watching Dad and me. "We have no time to waste."

An agonizing scream shattered the silence, and just as suddenly, it was cut off.

"What's going on?" I said. "Is anyone going to tell us?"

"Punishment," said Dorje. "Someone broke the rules and tried to harm us. The Imdura do not take it lightly."

"What kind of punishment?" I asked, not really wanting to know the answer.

Tashi was rigid, and her lips, almost bloodless, were pressed together as if she were trying hard to keep the words from spilling out. I had a feeling she disagreed with Dorje who ignored both of us.

Silently, we followed Dorje to a waterfall. It filled up a natural rock basin and flowed into an icy stream that plunged off the mountainside — a stark reminder that flat could turn to fall at any second. Definitely not a place to be wandering around in the dark. The sight of it filled me with dread. Thoughts of summer camp and the fiasco with Anjali flashed through my mind. I shuffled backward, keeping a healthy distance from the edge.

"There's our outdoor shower," said Dorje. "You can take a quick bath if you want."

The spray on my face was freezing. "You're joking," I said.

"Cold water is good for health and circulation," Dorje said. "I highly recommend it."

"No, thank you," I said through clenched teeth. "I'll wait till I get back home."

"I'm fine," said Dad, eyeing his camera sulkily.

"Okay," said Dorje with a shrug. He seemed to have forgotten the little incident from a few minutes ago and was almost jovial.

"Where does this lead?" I asked. "Is there a river close by?" It was good information to have handy.

"Yes, further down," said Dorje, pointing in the opposite direction. "But the forest is dangerous, and you must never wander here without a guide."

"You mean without someone to keep an eye on us," said Dad.

Now who's behaving like a spoiled child? Just because Dad couldn't take photos, he was being rude, but *I* had to be polite at all times. I felt sorry for him even though I hadn't forgiven him for the lie. After seeing what happened to someone who broke the rules, he needed to be careful. We both did.

"Let's go —" Dorje started to say.

"Someone's coming," Tashi cut in.

I strained my ears but heard nothing over the thundering waterfall. Even Dorje was narrowing his eyes and looking back the way we'd come. He lifted his hand, spear at the ready, and my stomach gurgled. Another attempt on our lives by the mysterious shadow? More rats and retribution?

Fie.

Norbu zipped out from the dense foliage and stood before us, panting.

"Your hearing's as good as a bat's," I said to Tashi, seriously impressed.

She shrugged as if the compliment didn't matter, but the tinge on her face told me she was pleased.

"What is it, Norbu?" said Dorje. "I thought I told you to stay with Shalva."

"Imma wants you all back now," Norbu replied, his sly eyes on me. What was it about Norbu that made me feel like I needed a good scrub whenever he was near?

"For the purification ceremony," he added.

"Purification ceremony?" Dad and I said in unison, glancing at each other.

Imdur was crawling with rats and they wanted to purify *the travelers*. I wanted to say something sarcastic, but I kept my lips clamped. Nervous laughter bubbled up inside, but I managed to contain it.

"Come," said Dorje. "You will find it very interesting."

"All right," said Dad, suddenly cheerful again. "Let's go."

The journey back was a lot faster. Dorje and Tashi set a brisk pace, though they were careful to keep an eye out.

I was soaked by the time we reached the village. The scream in the forest played over and over in my head, and Dad's sudden cheerfulness had my GF on high alert.

"Before we go to the ceremony, I need to drop into the guest house," said Dad. "I, er, would like to change into something more appropriate."

"Me too," I said, my stomach clenching painfully.

Dad was about to do something that would get us into serious trouble. I had to stop him before we were caught and punished.

CHAPTER 6

While Dorje waited outside the guest house, still hanging on to Dad's camera, we stepped inside to change. I saw that Dad had rigged up his tiny Quik-Pik camera to fit into a special shirt with a small opening sewn in, the remote to operate it in his trouser pocket. Once he wore a loose jacket over the top of his shirt, he could take pictures and no one would know. This looked like expensive surveillance equipment, and I had to hand it to Dad for being prepared. He was a professional at work, and a part of me grudgingly admired him.

A sour thought followed: he was so well prepared because this was not a camping trip, it was an assignment. He must have known that taking pictures openly might not be an option and had brought the surveillance camera. Another secret in this secret village. The Imdura were hiding things from us, and now Dad was hiding things from them. I'd agreed to this trip to get away from Anjali because of the secret we shared. The irony of all this did not escape me.

"They want privacy," I said, pulling on a dry T-shirt. "As their guests, shouldn't we respect their wishes?" I clipped the radio to my belt, unable to leave it behind.

"I'm doing this for you and your mother," Dad said. "Also, the world needs to know their story, and I'm going to be the one to tell it."

"And make a lot of money," I added bitterly. "Not to mention the fame."

Dad shrugged. "If I sold this for a good amount, I wouldn't have to take on so many assignments. I could spend more time at home. Your private school and our lifestyle are both expensive."

He had a point; like the Imdura, we could all learn to live without destroying our environment. But in doing so, he was going to expose them, against their will, and cash in on it. That part was very unfair, and yet I saw no way to stop him. It would be good to have him home more often. Maybe we could bond over a documentary just like I'd imagined. He might even get to like me the way I was and stop comparing me to Anjali.

"I'll meet you outside," I said, when Dad continued fiddling with the camera.

A chill breeze swept down the mountainside and into

the valley. Dorje hummed a tune under his breath while he waited. His eyes darted around, constantly surveying the surroundings.

"Dad will be out very soon," I said. "He had to use the bathroom."

Dorje nodded, examining Dad's full-size camera from every angle, even sniffing it.

"No explosives in there," I said, forcing a smile. "If that's what you are looking for."

"When are you planning to leave?" he asked suddenly.

I unclipped the radio from my belt and showed him the broken antenna. "As soon as I fix this and get a message over to the camp to come get us, or at least meet us halfway. Do you have a spare part I could use?"

"I'll fix it for you." He licked his lips as his hand closed around the radio. "Give it here."

I gripped the radio tight, trying not to shudder at the sight of Dorje's filthy hands and dirt-encrusted fingernails. We played tug-of-war, my GF urging me to hold on.

Dorje finally released it, grinning. "You're smart."

"Thanks, so are you," I said, attempting a smile, though my heart was pounding. The radio was our only link to the outside, and I wasn't letting it out of my sight for a *second*. "Why don't you bring the antenna to me and we'll repair it together?"

I thought he would argue, but he inclined his head and started humming again. It was the same melody I'd heard the night before. I secured the radio, hoping Tashi would be able to find me something to replace the broken part. I wasn't a book nerd for nothing, and the duct tape I'd brought would fix almost anything.

"All set!" said Dad, grinning, as he stepped out of the hut. The camera must be working well. Nothing but *that* could change his mood so drastically. If he got his pictures, we could be out of here by tomorrow.

Dorje's eyes lingered on Dad's shirt pocket. I sweated buckets. What if Dorje's eyesight was as good as his hearing?

THE ENTIRE VILLAGE, ABOUT two hundred and fifty strong, was gathered around the bamboo grove that seemed to be their community center.

The women wore colorful knee-length tunics and a lot of silver jewellery. Their hats were adorned with wildflowers that stuck out at all angles. The men, not to be outdone, wore maroon or green tunics with cummerbunds. Their hats had tassels that looked suspiciously like rats' tails. They all wore black rat fur coats. I'd left mine in the guest house and instead had donned three layers plus a jacket. It still wasn't as warm as the coat, and I regretted not wearing it.

A couple of drummers stood at the edge of the crowd.

One of them played with his drumstick, throwing it up in the air and catching it. He saw me looking at him and winked. His smile might have looked friendlier if not for the sharp, red-stained teeth. I smiled back, hoping I looked normal. My face felt frozen.

Gazing out at the sea of black coats, I wondered how many rats had died to provide warmth to the Imdura. And, more important, how many thousands still lurked in the village and forest.

The Imdura looked regal in black against a backdrop of snow-capped mountains and green bamboo forests. This picture was worth a million words, and Dad wasn't wasting a second. His hand in his pocket, he turned three hundred and sixty degrees, taking multiple photos of these strange people with their even stranger customs.

The villagers laughed and joked, creating a din. It was like being at the Chandni Chowk bazaar in Delhi on a Sunday. But underlying the chatter were those sounds again: high-pitched squeaks and clicks. I looked around, waiting for the rats to join the party. But not a tail nor a whisker was in sight.

As we walked through the crowd, it parted to let us through. The clicking grew louder, and I realized the villagers were speaking just like Dorje when he didn't want Dad and me to know what he was saying. I'd read about the African

Xhosa and their click language, but this did not sound like a language. At least, not a human language. If I closed my eyes, I saw a gigantic nest of rats in my head.

"Hello," I said politely to the villagers. My voice was thin and breathless, and I had to keep wiping my palms on my pants.

Some greeted me back. Others touched me. Their hands were rough and callused as they grazed my arm or cheek. I walked as fast as I could without sprinting. The combination of wet fur, decaying meat, and ammonia made my head swim and my eyes water.

Dorje pushed his way to the front of the crowd. I was hyperventilating. This was the first time I was seeing the entire village: sharp features, lean physiques, and tar-black eyes that followed me hungrily. These villagers needed more travelers to stop by, not fewer, so they could get used to visitors and not make such a big deal out of it or stare so rudely at Dad and me.

A low chant rippled through the crowd.

"Daazamus."

"Dasmus."

"Tazmus."

"Taazamaas."

What were they saying? I didn't understand it, and I didn't like it.

"Tashi!" I yelled, on the off chance that she'd be in the crowd. She was the one person who didn't make me nervous.

"It's okay, Krish," Dad said. "Just humour these guys. They must have so few travelers that every time someone stops by, they organize a ceremony. We're celebrities, as far as they're concerned."

I stared at Dad. Was he really that naive, or was he willing to ignore all the signs to get the pictures he wanted? We were not celebrities, but we were important in some way. I just hadn't figured out the how and why yet.

Observation 1: We were not welcome in the village. The only reason we were here was because we'd begged to stay.

Observation 2: They were keeping a close watch on us thanks to our shadows — Tashi and Dorje. One way to ensure we did not take any pictures.

Observation 3: This wasn't a celebration — it was a purification. Which implied we were tainted in some way. This was so rich, I almost smiled. Almost.

Observation 4: They believed we were dirtier than the rats, and in need of purification. How messed up was that?

"Tashi!" I called out again, my voice drowned by the chatter.

Suddenly she was beside me, and I couldn't help but gape. She wore a spotless white robe. Her silver hair, shimmering in the sun like a sheet of glass, hung loose over her shoulders, hiding most of the birthmark. A wide band of silver coins encircled her head, resting on her forehead. The top of the white staff she carried was carved in the shape of a rat.

"You look beautiful," I said, trying not to stammer.

"Really?"

I nodded. "Really."

She gave a tiny smile and touched the birthmark on her cheek. "Thank you," she whispered.

Ever since I'd saved her from getting squished, she'd been friendlier. I could use friendly right now. Somehow, I knew we were going to need help getting back to camp, and I hoped she would step up.

"What's going to happen at the ceremony, Tashi?"

"Imma will recite prayers and we'll eat *prasad* — sweets that have been blessed by our deity. The Imdura have to make sure that all travelers who stop here, even for a short time, are pure of heart and intention."

That ruled both Roys out. We were both rotten to the core: Dad was greedy, and I was his accomplice.

"If Imma finds us impure, does she make us clean the toilets?" I said, trying to make a joke of it. My pits dripped like a leaky tap, and my palms were sweaty even though my breath fogged in front of my face each time I spoke.

"We let the rats feed on you," she said.

I stopped so suddenly, Dad bumped into me. "Let's get this over with, Krish — I have lots to do."

I forced one foot in front of the other. "Don't people in Delhi tell jokes?" she said, smiling at what must be my horrified expression.

Before I could answer, we were at the grove, and the crowd closed up. We were hemmed in by the entire population of Imdur. The grove swarmed with rats, and Dad took photos, turning this way and that, smiling maniacally. If I hadn't been so scared, I would have told him to stop that because it would make the Imdura suspicious.

Instead, I crouched on the pretext of tying my shoelace and slipped a candy into my mouth.

Eight candies left.

CHAPTER 7

The sound of the drums, slow and deep, pulsed through the valley like a giant heartbeat. The villagers chanted in time. I wanted to push through the crowd and sprint all the way home to Delhi. But a tiny part of me was curious. I stayed where I was, watching, waiting.

"What happens next?" I whispered.

Tashi looked straight ahead, chanting with the rest. I shoved my clenched fists into my pockets and breathed deeply. I dared not look at the rats still erupting from their holes or I'd have run, screaming. I promised myself two candies if I got through this without fainting or having a meltdown.

Dad put a hand on my shoulder and squeezed. "Nothing to worry about, Krish. Just relax."

I moved closer to him so that our sides touched. It was slightly comforting.

The Imdura craned their heads, looking behind them. The crowd shifted restlessly. Imma was coming. She wasn't scary, even if this whole ceremony was a bit over the top. Why couldn't she have invited us to her hut, sprinkled us with holy water, and been done with it? What was the point of making such a big deal of our arrival?

Imma stepped through the crowd, a small but regal leader. Her silvery hair framed her serene face and fell to her waist. She, too, was in white from head to toe. A large red bindi nestled between her eyebrows, and a black strap circled her throat. It had two holes that looked like white eyes staring at me. Her headdress was an elaborate beehive of flowers and silver coins. It must have been heavy, but she seemed to float along without any signs of fatigue. My respect for her grew.

The shaman smiled at me as she approached. I smiled back and exhaled, unaware that I'd been holding my breath. This wasn't going to be so bad. Imma had made Dad back down. She was on my side. I had nothing to worry about. I even waved tentatively, and she nodded.

"Don't be fooled," Tashi said in the softest whisper. "She's a fraud."

I stared at her, surprised. Tashi frowned and shook her head.

Imma came up to us. Her eyes locked with mine, looking deep. She sniffed at me for a second or two with a funny expression. Was I stinking? I probably should have had a shower when Dorje showed us the waterfall. The last proper bath I'd had was at camp.

She walked over to Dad. After a cursory look and no sniff, Imma moved on. Not fair. Dad stank worse than I did. I noted that he didn't get a smile from her, either. She was still on my side, and that felt nice, sort of.

Imma spread her arms wide and said, "Welcome, travelers, Krish and Kabir Roy."

The crowd repeated her words, which seemed to echo around the valley. The drummers fell silent. I couldn't stop thinking about Tashi's warning about her mother, and I remembered her sadness when she'd asked about life in the city. Why couldn't she leave? Why did the Imdura not like travelers?

"We will start the ceremony," said Imma. "It will not take long, but it is important to me and my people." She said this while looking at Dad and me, as if we were in a position to refuse.

"Sure," said Dad. "We're game."

I shifted from one foot to the other, trying to ignore the hundreds of eyes on me. Dad loved the spotlight and continued taking photos. I agonized about the prasad Tashi had mentioned. It had better not be something gross. I didn't want to barf in front of an audience.

"Please sit down," said Imma.

"Where?" I asked.

Imma pointed to the ground, smirking. "Pick any spot that pleases your backsides."

Great. A smart aleck and a joker.

We sat down. I kept a wary eye out for the rats, which seemed to have retreated into the crowd or back in their holes. I looked up at the bamboo grove and immediately wished I hadn't. Pinpricks of light glowed within the shadows. I moaned softly.

"Deep breath, Krish," said Dad. "This will be over before you know it."

My mouth was so dry, I could barely swallow. There was no way I wouldn't "know" it. I was living this nightmare in cinematic color.

Imma took the rat-head staff from Tashi and thumped it on the ground three times, each time a little harder. Every time she thumped the staff, the crowd chanted as one.

Huh. Huh. Huh.

Imma kicked away her shoes, exposing pale feet with thick, yellow toenails sharpened to points. Barefoot, she sang and danced around us, wailing out a song that rose and fell. The villagers swayed and sang in unison as she danced. The words made no sense, but it sounded like a song of loss and grieving — a sad story. I wished I could understand the words, to get why they were happy and sad, even though it was quite painful to hear.

I turned toward Tashi. She was gone. Eyes glued to a distant mountain peak, I set up my own chant.

I can do this. Huh.

I can do this. Huh.

I will do this. Ha, ha, ha.

As soon as Imma stopped singing, the villagers fell silent, too. She came up to me and touched the bottom of the staff to my head, then my right and left shoulders, and finally my chest. Black goo was stuck to it, and I couldn't help thinking of germs. It felt as if someone had set me on fire. Good thing I was sitting, or I would have fallen in a dead faint.

I can do this. I will do this.

Imma went through the same motions with Dad, but faster. I guessed she didn't like him very much, and that made me happy. For once, someone preferred boring, nerdy, unathletic me to my famous, talented, athletic dad.

"Bring the prasad," Imma called out.

The crowd parted. Tashi and Norbu hurried to the front, carrying a large clay plate of steaming bread with a bowl of white paste in the center of it. They put it down in front of Dad and me.

"I can't eat all of this!" I said, staring at the plate. "I'll burst!"

Imma laughed. "The bread is not for you."

Tashi looked at me, hard, almost as if she were offering me strength. Then she backed away and stood beside Imma. The bread was fresh and smelled delicious. If this was the blessed food, I'd be happy to take two helpings. I'd barely completed the thought when I heard a squeak. It was joined by another and then another.

The chorus turned into a crescendo.

"Stay seated," roared Imma, her bare feet firmly planted on the ground. "If you stand up, you have darkness in your hearts."

I didn't care about having the blackest heart in the universe, or a black hole for a heart, because no way was I remaining seated with rats charging at me. Dad must have been thinking the same thing, because we both leaped to our feet just as a flood of rats converged on the food.

They poured over Imma's feet — a seething black river of fur, claws, and teeth.

If I fainted, it would be like diving into a pool of rats. Sheer willpower and paralyzing fear kept me on my feet.

CHAPTER 8

The rats ranged in size from tiny to enormous. They pounced on the bread and ripped it to shreds with razor-sharp teeth. Many swarmed over my boots. A large, hairy one scrambled up my pants, and man did he stink — exactly like the fur coat I'd snuggled into these last couple of days.

I stomped my foot, and the rat fell off. The crowd booed. I started a countdown: one thousand, nine hundred and ninety-nine, nine hundred and ninety-eight …

The crowd hemmed us in. Even if we could have run, it would have been a huge mistake. I had to see this through. The rats chattered as they devoured the bread. Some let out high-pitched screams. It was like being in a waking nightmare.

Dad faced the shaman and the villagers, clicking away with the camera in his pocket. He was lucky there was such a din at the ceremony, or someone would have heard the camera shutter. He was getting the story of a lifetime while

I was trying not to faint. I was so mad at Anjali and Naveen Uncle for being at Adventure Camp. If they hadn't joined us, I would never have wanted to get away on this side trip. A part of me knew this was crap, but I needed somewhere to channel my anger so I would forget to be scared.

Imma knelt before the rats, her eyes closed. She prayed softly, rocking back and forth. Rats swarmed over her, blobs of black on her white clothes. They scurried to the top of her head and back down. Some gripped her hair and face with their claws, squeaking softly. She squeaked back. A few bold ones perched on her head, their tails hanging over her face like a pink veil.

I dug my nails into my palms. The pain kept me on my feet.

The villagers were on their knees, praying along with the shaman. Only Dad and I were still standing. The rats stared at me. Hundreds, thousands of them. Their dank, musky stink enveloped me, and their screams rose to a painful clamour.

As soon as the bread was gone, the rats retreated.

Imma opened her eyes and stood up. Tashi hurried forward with her mother's shoes and helped her put them on. Imma stroked Tashi's hair. "My child, it'll soon be your turn to lead our people, and no one will be prouder than I to hand over the staff."

Tashi jerked away from Imma, who clicked her tongue

in irritation. *What was going on between the two?* I couldn't wait to ask Tashi about it as well as her cryptic warning about her mother.

Imma dipped the end of her staff into the paste. Shalva, seated up front, held out his hands. Imma smeared a bit of paste on them. He touched his palms to his forehead and ate the paste.

"May the Imdura never go hungry again!" Shalva said in a quavering voice.

"Never go hungry again!" Imma repeated after him, and all the villagers joined in except Tashi. She stood quietly, watching them with a sad expression.

"I offer the blessings of Shubra-Musa to each and every one of you," said Imma, raising her voice. "Come forth. This time, our guests will approach last."

The villagers lined up in front of Imma. My head pounded. My stomach gurgled. I could not eat something the rats had used as a dance floor seconds ago. I'd rather be thrown out of the village and take my chances with wild animals and the mystery shadow in the forest.

The line grew shorter. So did my breath. Each villager took a little prasad, said a brief prayer, and licked it up. I met Tashi's eyes. She looked pained and apologetic. But she didn't say a word; she wouldn't go against her mother's wishes. I had to speak up, no matter the consequences.

"Rats carry germs and diseases," I yelled out when there were only a couple of people ahead of me. "They must be killed, or you will all die of the plague. Don't eat that paste!"

Dad scrabbled to take his hands out of his pockets to shut me up, but he was too late. Hostile looks zinged my way.

"Please forgive my son," said Dad. "He's been very upset since we got lost. I apologize on his behalf."

I glared at Dad. His dedication to his photography was admirable, but eating contaminated food without protest was taking it too far.

Imma took an extra-large helping of paste from the plate and came up to me. "Hold out your hand, Krish," she said in a soft voice. The steel in her eyes could have been industrial grade.

I shook my head. I wasn't giving up common sense and hygiene just to please her.

"You are disrespecting us by refusing," she said. "You will eat this now, or you will face the consequences."

"I'm sorry, but no." There were black flecks in the paste. I clamped my hands to my mouth and backed away, hoping, praying, I wouldn't barf on her.

Tashi squeezed herself between us. "I will eat the prasad on his behalf, Imma. It is also our custom to respect our guests' wishes. They're avatars of Shubra-Musa, right?"

Imma flushed, and I thought she was going to strike us both. Instead, she smiled. It wasn't friendly. "Thank you for reminding me of our customs, daughter."

She looked over at Dad. "Would you like some prasad, or would you prefer that someone else get the blessing of our ancestors?"

Dad shuffled forward and held out his trembling hands. Imma smeared a large dollop of paste into his cupped palms. Dad closed his eyes and put the paste in his mouth. I was sure I heard him gagging, but he masked it with a cough.

Tashi extended her hands and got a double portion of the paste. She touched it to her forehead, murmured a prayer, and swallowed the lot.

Imma looked at Dad and me. "You have been purified. Others who did not understand the importance of the ceremony ran screaming. Though you did not remain seated, you did not run away. For that, I and our ancestors thank you."

Ancestors? I looked around, wondering if I'd missed the ghosts. A tiny black nose peeked over Imma's shoulder. She raised a hand and stroked it.

Right, those ones.

"There's a full moon in two days' time — a special occasion for us," Imma continued. "We've planned a feast for the following day, and you will be our guests of honour."

I didn't bother telling her that we wouldn't be here two

days from now. At least, I wouldn't. If Dad wanted to stay, he was welcome. I was taking the radio and leaving. I was counting on getting a message to camp, so help might arrive before I had to take any drastic measures. I'd memorized the coordinates Dad and I had discussed yesterday when we'd tried to figure out where Imdur lay on the map.

Tashi walked with me back to the guest house after the ceremony.

"You're a lifesaver!" I told her.

She shrugged.

"I want to give you something," I said and pulled out a candy from my pocket, unwrapped it, and placed it on her palm. I took out two for myself. I had five left, and I'd have to ration them. But Tashi deserved one for saving me from embarrassing myself in front of the villagers.

"What do I do with this?" she asked, prodding the red lump with her finger. She sniffed it and looked up, confused.

"Eat it," I said, cramming my two in my mouth.

She ate hers and smiled. "Very tasty."

"Better than the prasad, right?"

She frowned. "You should not make fun of our customs. They may not make sense to you, but they do to us. You have to respect our ways."

"You had trouble too," I said. "Why did you say 'don't be fooled' earlier and that your mother was a fraud?

"I shouldn't have said that," she replied. "Forget about it."

I was taking a huge risk, confessing my fear to the sha-man's daughter — but I needed to get it out or I'd burst. "I can't," I said. "I have a feeling we're in terrible danger."

Tashi jerked as if she'd stepped on a piece of glass.

"Please tell me what's going on!"

She hesitated. I sweated. If she bailed on me now and went running to her mother, I was dead. Imma would punish me first, and Dad would work on what was left of me for ruining his photography session.

"You are in danger," she whispered finally, eyes darting around her.

I knew it! "You're somehow in league with the rats, right? You worship them and feed them. Why?"

"Not now," she said, walking more quickly.

"Then tonight?" I had to know what we were up against.

"Not tonight, but I will come to you as soon as I can. Stay indoors. And don't break any rules — that's very important. We live by rules, and punishment is severe."

Her eyes locked with mine, and they looked intense. I could tell she was deeply unhappy and worried about some-thing. If I could help her in some way, she would help me. But the reminder of the punishment scared me.

As Tashi walked away, something Imma had said nagged at me.

Others ran screaming.

Others did not eat the prasad.

How many *others* had there been?

And more importantly, where were they now?

CHAPTER 9

"You could have gotten us killed, or thrown out of the village," said Dad the minute he returned to the guest house. "What were you thinking, refusing their food?"

Ignoring him, I flopped on the bed and stared out the window. I'd once thought the Ladakh Range was majestic. Now the snow-capped mountains looked like a prison, with bars of bamboo.

Dad's face hovered over me. "Are you listening to me, Krish?"

"Yes."

"I need your help these next two days. I have to get lots of photographs. Please don't mess things up for me now."

How could he worry more about his photos than about me, his own son?

Dad scrolled through the pictures he'd taken at the ceremony, grinning. I wanted to yell at him to take this situation, to take me, seriously. But I knew it wouldn't make any difference.

When he was done, Dad sat beside me. "I know this is hard, Krish. And truth be told, that prasad was pretty gross."

"Why didn't you refuse it? Are these photos more important than your health? Our safety? I've been telling you I get a bad feeling about this place, and you keep ignoring me."

"You're letting your imagination get the better of you again, Krish. Nothing is going to happen to us. Besides, Kabir Roy has never slipped up on an assignment. It's a personal guarantee, and when people approach me, they know I will not fail them."

But you'll fail me, because I'm not that important to you.

The realization was crushing. I swept the painful thought aside and tried to reason with him. "How do you know you're the first to be asked to do this assignment? Imma said there were others."

"There you go again, imagining dangers that aren't there," said Dad, his voice sharp. "We're safe here. The Imdura may be living in a remote area with weird customs, but they're not about to cook us in a stew." He chuckled. "At the end of our stay, you'll be tougher than before. I guarantee it."

"Like Anjali, you mean?" I couldn't keep the bitterness out of my voice.

"Well, she did attend a wilderness boot camp for two weeks, but you're not there yet. Baby step—"

I ran out the door, slamming it behind me. I was sick of

the same old story. *I* needed to be more like Anjali — never that she needed to be more like me. It had been okay — sort of — when Anjali and I were best friends and she took my side. Now, I had no one in my corner.

"Krish, wait!" Dad called out from the window. "I'm sorry, I know you hate being compared, but *you* brought up Anjali's name. Can we please talk?"

I ran to get as far away from him as possible. The village hummed with life as the Imdura went about their daily chores: cleaning their homes, collecting firewood, and using bamboo to make baskets, vessels, furniture. Some tended vegetable patches covered with wire mesh.

The central area was the busiest. Smoke rose from six wood-fired pits. Men and women worked there, filling lengths of bamboo with uncooked rice, meat, and vegetables. The inevitable rats scurried around them, giving the fires a wide berth.

The Imdura chattered and laughed as they worked, not the least bit ashamed of their odd clothing, customs, or language. No one gave them a hard time about who they were except people like us: outsiders.

I scrambled up a tiny hillock. It gave a good view of the village, the bamboo grove, and the mountains. If Anjali had been here with us, things would have been so different. For one, Dad would have been nicer.

I couldn't help but remember summer, last year. Anjali had signed up for camp and insisted I join too. She promised she would help me get over my fears. I believed her. During a scorching afternoon when we were all supposed to be indoors, playing games, Anjali and I had sneaked to the lake to cool off. I waded and splashed in the shallows, while she swam further away from shore where it was deeper. Suddenly she screamed for help, sobbing that she had a cramp. I stood there, paralyzed. I hadn't been able to get over my fear of water enough to learn how to swim. Now my best friend was drowning, and I couldn't help her.

Anjali was in so much pain, she could barely move her legs. She begged me to come in and save her. But the water was deep — and full of germs. I turned into a coward and ran away. Luckily, the mess tent was close by and one of the cooks heard her screaming. She rescued Anjali.

We did not speak for the duration of that camp. Each time I approached her to explain why I'd run, she walked away. I was so miserable, I wanted to call Mom to pick me up early. But I would have had to explain why. I gritted my teeth and stayed.

Since then, Anjali was polite when we met at family gatherings, but I missed the old Anjali. She'd always had my back, but the one time she'd needed me the most, I'd failed her.

What must she be doing right now? Would she be worried that we hadn't communicated with them in two days? Without a radio I would never know. I had to try to get it working. Dad wasn't concerned, and it was up to me.

A couple of kids playing beside their hut caught my eye. They'd arranged marbles in a circle on the ground and were taking turns to strike them with more marbles. A bamboo box beside them overflowed with odds and ends. I might find something to repair the radio in that jumble. I hurried down the hillock toward them.

"Hi!" I said, kneeling and glancing into the box.

The boys looked at me.

"May I join you?"

The younger one shook his head. The older one just stared.

I was getting suspicious looks from a few Imdura. I'd have to work fast before someone came over to ask questions. "You have anything like this?" I pointed to the broken antenna on the radio, still clipped to my belt.

"No," said the older boy.

"I'll just take a peek in your toy box, okay?" I hid the radio and emptied the box onto the ground without the boys' permission, feeling like a bully and a jerk. But I was desperate. I needed to get the radio working.

"Stop!" said the older boy.

I ignored him, sifting through the odds and ends: a set of dentures, a disposable camera, a battery, an elastic hairband, and few Lego pieces. Nothing I could use. *Where had all this come from?*

"I'm happy to see you mingling with us," said a soft voice behind me. I jumped up to see Imma smiling at me.

How did the Imdura manage to move so quietly? Tashi, Dorje, and now the shaman, who had managed to creep up on me even though she was wearing enough metal to anchor a ship!

"I like that you do not stick to the guest house and are getting to know the Imdura," she said. "Maybe you'll stay with us forever?"

Panic shot through me. "No, thanks. I want to go home. My mother is waiting, and school starts again in a few days."

"You can school here," she said, glancing at the litter on the ground. "Looks like you're searching for something. What do you want?"

My GF tingled. I didn't dare tell her the truth. "Looking for a spare battery for my flashlight," I said in a burst of inspiration, hoping the boys wouldn't rat me out. Luckily, they had become mute in the presence of their leader.

"I see," she said. Her eyes did that X-ray thing again, looking straight into me. Could she tell I was lying? That I had a black hole for a heart?

"Come, join me for tea," said Imma. "I'd like to talk to you. I can sense that you need to get a few things off your chest. Hmmm?"

"Dad is waiting for me."

"But you were playing with your new friends, so obviously you're not in a hurry to get back. Right?"

She was sharp. I hesitated, trying to come up with another excuse.

She stepped closer, her gray eyes staring into mine. "Come, I have something you desperately need."

Was Imma a mind reader? If anyone in the village had an antenna, it would be her. I'd pop in, be polite, see what she had lying around, and get out fast. Easy as snapping my fingers.

"Okay," I said. I wanted to avoid drinking or eating anything gross and wondered how I would do it politely.

The roof of Imma's hut was covered with emerald-green moss. Some of the bamboo stakes in the walls were sprouting leaves. It was as if the hut were still breathing, still growing. The clay dish outside the door was half full of paste. A small rat lay still beside it, paws in the air.

Imma gave a little cry and lunged forward. She scooped up the rat in her palms and sniffed. My skin crawled. I kept my distance. She opened the rat's mouth, brought it close to hers, and blew into it. The rat didn't twitch a whisker.

Mouth-to-mouth resuscitation on a filthy rat. Gross.

"Gone," whispered Imma. A tear trickled down her face.

"It's just a rat," I said and knew, instantly, it was the wrong thing to say aloud.

Her face twisted into an ugly expression. "It could be your relative. Or mine. Rats are people, reincarnated. Once they have paid their dues in the lowly rat form, they come back as humans. Don't you ever disrespect them again."

Agreeing to join her had been a stupid idea. I would be at the mercy of this shaman who thought rats were her relatives.

"I know you think I'm mad," said Imma, as if she'd read my thoughts. She pushed open the intricately carved door. "That we all are. You will come to understand our ways if you open your heart and mind."

We stepped into a narrow corridor with a bench and pegs along the wall. Imma took off her shoes and gestured to me to do the same. The thought of walking around in my socks with rats underfoot wasn't appealing, but to wear outdoor shoes in someone's living space is disrespectful no matter where you are. I unlaced my boots and left them by the bench.

Most people collect mugs, plates, masks, even, to display on the walls of their homes. Imma collected skulls. I stood for a few seconds, staring at the corridor walls filled with skulls of every shape and size. As my eyes adjusted to the gloom, the weird shapes took form. Rat skulls. It was like being in a horror museum.

I followed Imma to the living room. The air was fragrant with herbs and spices. A fire burned in the hearth, and Shalva sat beside it, knitting. He ignored us, his hands moving automatically.

"Hello, Shalva," I said, politely.

Shalva grunted, his eyes still on the knitting.

"Shalva is the oldest in our village," said Imma. "And when he's in the mood, he can tell the best stories about our ancestors and how we came here."

"Where were you before Imdur?" I asked.

"We moved here from Mizoram to escape Mautam — bamboo death," said Imma. "It's an interesting story. Would you like to hear it?"

I nodded. I was intrigued, especially with the death part. "Er, where's Tashi, by the way?"

"Collecting herbs for tonight," said Shalva in a creaky voice.

"Make yourself comfortable," said Imma. "I'll be back with the tea after I take care of this innocent one." She still had the dead rat cradled in her palm.

I wanted to remind her to wash her hands after she'd taken care of it. I kept my mouth shut. Nothing good could come out of making her mad at me.

As soon as she'd gone, Shalva put the knitting down. "Help me up," he commanded.

I shuffled over, not keen to touch him but unable to refuse to help an old man. Shalva grasped my wrist tight and pulled himself up, almost knocking me off my feet. I tried not to shudder at his touch, which was sandpapery.

His cloudy eyes cleared momentarily. He looked at me and pinched my cheek. "I can see why she likes you. You'll make a fine Imdura when you become one of us."

CHAPTER 10

I jumped back so fast, I crashed into a low stool and fell over. Was Shalva mad? No way was I staying in this ghastly little village with its rats and secrets.

"What do you mean?" I asked.

"I need to lie down," said Shalva, his eyes cloudy again. He shuffled to a door leading to the back of the house and walked away without a backward glance.

I had to leave, not just Imma's home but the village. It felt as if the mountains had taken a step closer, crowding in on me. But first I had to find something to repair the radio. I could do this if I stayed calm.

Look around. Find something. Get out!

An assortment of bamboo furniture filled the room. I moved fast, peering at the shelves of glass bottles with herbs and potions of every imaginable color. Something caught my eye, and I stepped closer. A large glass jar had an albino rat floating in it. Its red eyes stared into mine. I rubbed my arms, trying to control my nausea.

Odd knick-knacks adorned every spare inch of wall. There was a ski, a cracked pair of ski goggles, a backpack, a water-damaged copy of *The Lion, the Witch, and the Wardrobe*. Even a pair of glasses on a silver chain. Whom did these belong to? Where were the owners now?

Others. These articles might have belonged to the others. There was an open spot on the wall. What was Imma planning to put up there?

I pushed the thought out of my head and focused on my search. A glint beside the fireplace caught my eye: Shalva's knitting needles. I hurried over, my eyes darting toward the door. Imma could return at any minute.

With a sweaty hand I eased a needle from the ball of wool. It almost slipped and clattered to the floor. I caught it in time and stuffed it into one of my pant pockets. I turned the ball of wool over so the missing needle wouldn't be spotted immediately. For good measure, I threw a shawl over it.

There was no sign of Imma. Time for me to get out. The albino rat floating in the jar seemed to be glaring at me. I closed my eyes, breathed deeply, and hurried to the door.

I scooped up my boots and was about to tiptoe out when Imma entered the living room carrying a tray with two cups, a steaming teapot, and a plate of flat buns.

"Surely you're not running away without a word," said

Imma. Her voice was soft, barely above a whisper, but it carried her displeasure.

I shrugged. "I have things to do."

"Don't we all? Stay for a while. It will do you good, and I would love your company."

I admit I was flattered. Dad had never said he loved my company, nor was I keen on another argument.

"All right," I said and perched on the edge of a stool. How was I going to eat buns that were most likely contaminated? But how could I refuse without making her mad at me?

Imma sat cross-legged on a cushion and poured tea. The fragrance of bamboo flowers and lemon perfumed the air. She offered me a bun. I stared at it, sweat oozing from every pore.

"I can't," I said. The memory of her displeasure when I'd refused the prasad flashed through my mind. "I'm so sorry, but I really can't. My stomach is very ... ummm ... delicate." It was lame, but it was the best I could do.

"I know just what will help." Imma fetched a glass bottle filled with bright orange shavings from a shelf and shook some into one of the cups of tea. A citrusy smell lingered in the air even after she stoppered the bottle. "Drink up," she said. "It will reduce the anxiety hanging over you all the time, like a black cloud."

I sniffed the contents of the cup and took a sip. The hot

liquid scalded my tongue. I swallowed quickly. Lemons, oranges, and something bitter exploded in my mouth. My gut burned, and I was sure she'd poisoned me. What a fool I'd been. As suddenly as the sensation had appeared, it was gone. A cozy warmth spread through me. It felt as if my body, wound tight like a corkscrew, was finally unfurling. Relaxing.

"Better?" said Imma.

I nodded, reached for a bun, and devoured it. "What are those orange shavings?"

"A special plant that grows only in this forest," said Imma. "It's a calming herb."

I ate another sweet-salty bun and washed it down with tea. "It's good stuff. Can I have some to take with me?" Even though I had sanitizer in my pocket, I had no desire to slather my hands.

Imma laughed. "If you stay with us, you can have an endless supply."

I laughed too. She was so funny! "Is this the stuff Tashi has gone to collect in the forest?"

"That and something for the ceremony tonight," said Imma, watching me.

"You have a ceremony for everything," I said, unable to stop laughing. "Do you have one for going to the bathroom?" My laughter died away when Imma did not join in.

"I'd like to hear the bamboo death story," I said, changing the topic. Also, I really was curious.

"Finish your tea first," she said.

The fire crackled and the room smelled of oranges. It felt like walking through a farmer's market on a hot summer day, the smells of fresh fruit perfuming the air. I was so relaxed, I almost toppled from the stool. Imma pointed to a cushion on the floor. I slid down and sat cross-legged beside her, leaning back to stare at the bamboo ceiling. I could have fallen asleep right there.

"Believe in yourself," said Imma, suddenly. "Own who you are even if it's weird or different from what people expect you to be."

How did she know what Dad and I had argued about? That I longed for Dad to say precisely those words to me? Her eyes were kind, gentle.

"It's not so easy," I said, gulping more tea. "In school and at home, everyone expects you to fit in, not stand out."

"Being different is *never* easy," she said, leaning back and sipping her tea. "Take us, for example. Imdur is not on any map. We have no electricity or internet. The forest gives us almost everything we need, so we rarely go into the city. And we worship rats. Every traveler who discovers our village and shelters here for a day or two thinks we're strange. We are what we are, and it has taken us a hundred and fifty years to not care about what the world thinks of us."

"Where are those travelers now?"

"Gone," she said, fluttering her fingers. "We don't like outsiders here just as much as they don't like to linger here. They miss their fancy gadgets and being connected with people they hardly know through the internet. The only connection you need is with yourself, with your loved ones, and with nature. We have all that here." Her face was serene, contented.

"Why rats?" I said. "You're all educated and know what they're capable of."

Imma laughed. It was deep and genuine. I couldn't help but laugh too. "Not these ones. Plague is caused because of the conditions in which the rats live, what they eat, how they breed. In Imdur, we feed them what we eat. We live in clean surroundings untouched by pollution and chemicals. No one in Imdur has died because of the rats in years. Not since the last Mautam in 1863."

"Mautam — the bamboo death," I said, stuffing another bun in my mouth. "Sounds mysterious."

She sighed deeply. "It is a long story, and I will tell you when we have more time. All I will say now is that at one time we were at war with the rats. It was us against them, and they were winning. Now we are one with them. We live in complete harmony. Come, you must help me with a very important ceremony." Her eyes twinkled.

I laughed. She was teasing me because I'd made a joke about there being a ceremony for everything. I followed her to the backyard. It was fenced in and had a vegetable patch on one side. The rest of it was bare with numerous holes. The dead rat lay by the door.

"Pick it up and bury it," said Imma.

I stared at it, my skin prickling. My body was reluctant, but my brain egged it on.

"Go on," said Imma. "I've told you, they're clean. You wouldn't hesitate to help a human baby, would you? A baby rat is no different."

Imma's voice was soothing, almost hypnotic. I picked it up and examined it. It *was* just a baby, with pink nose and paws, and so soft. Tears welled up in my eyes as it lay lifeless on my palm.

Imma led me to one of the holes. I knew what I had to do. I lay the rat gently into the hole and scooped mud over it till it was covered. Imma murmured a prayer as she circled the grave clockwise, then counter-clockwise. Tears spilled down my cheeks as I wiped my muddy hands on my pants. It felt so good to be normal. To forget about germs. I smiled through my tears.

"Krish!"

I jumped to my feet, almost knocking Imma over.

Tashi burst into the backyard. "What are you doing?"

"The future shaman should show restraint," said Imma in a cold voice. "Stop yelling."

"We buried a baby rat," I said, tears still leaking from my eyes. "It was so sweet, and now it's dead. Maybe it'll come back as my aunty." I wiped my face on my sleeve. "Or your uncle."

"Shalva is asking for you," said Tashi, glaring at Imma. "Now."

Imma frowned as she hurried past Tashi into the hut. "Come back soon, Krish. We have so much to discuss."

"Can I have some more of that herb?" I called out.

"No," said Imma with a laugh. "You'll have to come to see me if you want more."

I didn't like the sound of that.

"Tashi, take Krish back to the guest house and come right back. We have to prepare for the initiation ceremony tonight." Imma waved and hurried inside.

"I've brought your boots," said Tashi. "We'll go through the backyard."

I put on my boots and hurried after her. Once again, it felt like an entire conversation had taken place between mother and daughter in a silent language.

"What's the hurry?" I asked. "And what's wrong? Are you mad at me?"

Tashi dragged me outside. "Do you realize you were handling a dead rat and crying?"

"I was?" I asked, searching her face. My head was starting to throb, and my mouth was dry and cottony. "Why? How?"

"I don't have time to explain now, but you have to leave as soon as possible. I'll help you." Her gray eyes held fear.

"But she was nice to me," I said. "She calmed me down so I could eat without worrying about germs."

"It was the herbs in your tea," Tashi replied. "She could give you something that would make you leap off the mountaintop, and you'd do it laughing."

Whatever was in the herbs was wearing off quickly. Anxiety exploded inside me — like an airbag after a car crash.

"Our radio is busted," I said. "I stole your grandfather's knitting needle. Don't tell him."

Tashi looked at me solemnly when we reached the guest house. "Stay indoors tonight and try to get that radio working. It's your best chance of getting out of here alive. Hurry!"

"Thank you," I said. "You're amazing."

She gave me a tiny smile and raced away, her silver hair shimmering in the sunlight. I went inside, trying to make sense of her warning. Imma wanted me to stay; her daughter wanted us to leave. Whom should I believe?

My GF broke the tie. I was going with Tashi's warning.

CHAPTER 11

"Where have you been, Krish?" Dad asked. "I was starting to get worried."

"Tashi said we should leave as soon as possible. We're in danger." I hoped Dad would take this more seriously if it came from one of the Imdura instead of me.

Dad frowned. "Now there's another child with a lot of imagination. We made a deal, Krish — I get two days here, and then we leave. I expect a man to keep his word."

I felt sick. Still, I had to warn him, to keep him safe.

"There's an initiation ceremony tonight. That's why Tashi couldn't stay to tell me more, but she insisted we stay indoors and not break any rules. She said the Imdura, but especially her mother, are big on rules. No pictures, Dad, but the great news is that I found a spare part. If we can repair the radio this evening while the Imdura are at the ceremony, we can contact Adventure Camp. Don't you think Anjali and Naveen Uncle will be worried about us?"

"Another ceremony?" he said, his eyes lighting up. "Good work, Krish!"

"That's all you heard?" I shook my head, unable to believe his recklessness. "Dad, listen to me. It's not safe to leave the guest house except to use the bathroom. You have to believe me!"

"Please stop shouting," said Dad. "You're obviously out of your comfort zone and prone to believing anything that is said. I doubt there would be very serious consequences if we were caught."

"I'm working on the radio," I said, pulling the needle from my pocket. He wasn't going to listen to anything I said, so what was the point of wasting my breath?

"I'll take a quick look around and be right back," said Dad. He hurried out the door and was gone without a backward glance.

Being ignored was hard. I missed Anjali terribly right then. Not only would she have understood, but she would have taken me seriously. If I ever had another chance to make things up to Anjali, I would be much braver. I wouldn't hesitate for a second.

I laid out the repair kit, the knitting needle, and the duct tape on my bed. The light outside was fading, but the village was livelier than ever. Fires glowed orange against the deep blue sky. The chattering of the rats echoed around the village. I was safer in here than out there, but where was Dad?

For the next hour I worked steadily, sweat burning my eyes, my ears pricked up for any sign of Dad returning — I was hoping he wouldn't get caught.

Finally, the sound of footsteps. Something coiled tight inside me loosened. Dad returned with Dorje, who'd brought dinner. We were to eat in here and weren't invited to join the village tonight. What kind of initiation were they preparing for? A part of me understood Dad's curiosity, but not his recklessness.

"Can I help with the radio?" Dorje asked, setting the tray on the table.

I'd hid the needle as soon as I heard the door open. "Thanks, but I've got it," I replied. "You sure you have no way of travelling somewhere? What if there's an emergency?"

"We have everything we want here. When we need to go to Leh, we walk there. It's a brisk three-day walk," Dorje replied.

"Do you think I'm lying?" he said when I did not reply.

Yes, I thought. *I think you're lying.* What if a person was too sick to walk? Surely they had a faster means of travel.

"What's going on this evening?" Dad asked casually. "Everyone seems very excited."

"A young boy becomes a man," said Dorje. He smelled

riper than usual, and I wondered if he'd been pulling my leg about using the outdoor shower. He needed it more than we did.

"Can we watch?" Dad asked. "I find Imdur and its customs fascinating."

"This is a sacred ceremony, and outsiders are forbidden to participate or watch," said Dorje. "Please do not leave the guest house. We will see you at breakfast tomorrow."

Dad blanched but managed a friendly smile. "Sure. Good night."

"We'll probably be on our way tomorrow," I said with more conviction than I felt. "You won't have to worry about keeping an eye on us or following us around."

Dorje gave me an odd look. "Good night," he said and walked away.

Dad and I ate dinner silently. Good thing he'd decided not to scold me about that last statement to Dorje. But my frustration was slowly turning to anger, and I was at the end of my patience with Dad, who still refused to take me seriously.

"You're not going to disobey him, are you?" I said when I'd finished dinner.

"I can't squander this opportunity, Krish. Come with me! If the ceremony in the morning was any indication, this one will be fascinating too."

The thought of leaving the guest house at night, with the

rats out in full force, made my stomach lurch. "No, thanks. I'm going to take Tashi's and Dorje's advice. You should too."

"If I get some great shots, I'll have enough footage for a feature story," said Dad, as if I hadn't spoken at all. "We can leave tomorrow and tell the camp guys to meet us halfway. Okay?"

It was a losing battle. He was going no matter what, and I might as well accept it. With any luck, he'd get what he needed, and we'd be out of here. "Okay. But what if I can't get the radio to work? We can't tell the camp staff anything if we can't talk to them."

"We'll leave and try to find our way back anyway," said Dad. "The main thing is we'll be out of here and on our way home. That's what you want, right? To get out of Imdur?"

"Yes, as soon as we can. This place terrifies me, Dad."

"Then let's get on with our jobs, shall we?" said Dad. For the rest of the evening, he fiddled with his camera, testing it for night shots. I'd attempted to reinforce the broken antenna with the knitting needle so that it could still be extended to the fullest height. I hoped the careful use of duct tape wouldn't interfere with the reception. After an hour, I was done.

I switched it on. Nothing. Adjusting the antenna height, I moved closer to the window and opened it a crack. Even if the reception wasn't clear, there should be some static.

Nothing but silence.

"It's not working," I said, trying to control the tremble in my voice. Had I broken something more delicate inside? I clicked it on and off in quick succession. I even thumped it.

Dad ruffled my hair. "It's okay, Krish. Take it easy and get some rest. We'll figure it out in the morning."

I hugged the radio to my chest and lay down. Dad stretched out on the bed too. Outside, the revelry became louder. And yet, I drifted off.

A noise woke me. My eyes snapped open and my pulse accelerated. A shadow moved beside Dad's bed. I almost yelled out but caught myself in time. It was Dad, getting ready to head out. Cold dread seeped through me.

"Don't go, Dad. Please. I have a bad feeling about this. It's not safe."

"Krish, *I* know how to take care of myself." I heard the unspoken words: *unlike you.*

"Do you even know where this ceremony is taking place? Everything they do is a secret."

"I overheard the location when I took a walk," said Dad, concealing the tiny camera he'd used this morning. "Some-one mentioned a temple in the forest." He continued to work, secure in the knowledge that he'd gotten away with it once and could easily do it again.

"Dad, please don't go!" I grabbed his arm and hung on.

"You can't have forgotten that Dorje sent rats after whoever threw the boulder at us. You can't go, Dad. *Please*."

Someone knocked. We'd both forgotten the Imdura's excellent hearing.

Dad brushed my hand off and opened the door. Dorje stood there, dressed in black from head to toe. His lips were tinged red. He'd either been drinking beet juice or eating rare steak. My GF bet on the latter.

"Why are you two still awake?" said Dorje, his eyes darting between us.

"Why are you outside the guest house at this time of night?" asked Dad, none too politely.

Dorje scratched his nose. "I was passing by and heard loud voices."

Dad glanced at his watch. "At one in the morning?"

Dorje's eyes swept over us. "I don't sleep well, so I walk. Good night."

"I'm not sleepy either," said Dad. "Why don't we walk together?"

Dorje shut the door in our faces. There was an audible click as a key turned.

"He's locked us in. Happy?"

"There are more ways than one to slip out," Dad said, his face grim. "What are they hiding from us? Now I *have* to find out their secret."

Dad slammed the back door shut. We waited a few minutes, listening hard. I didn't expect to hear anything, though. The Imdura were silent and stealthy, just like the rats.

"That's more than enough time for Dorje to go around to the back," Dad whispered. "Go to sleep, I'll be back before you know it. I promise we'll leave tomorrow." He squeezed my shoulder, climbed through the window, and dropped down. He looked both ways and hurried away into the darkness.

Dad was making a huge mistake, but I couldn't stop him. I was scared and angry now. If something happened to him because of his recklessness, I'd be left here, alone. How was I going to get back home with the radio busted? I had to watch his back. And that meant I couldn't lie in bed.

I dressed as fast as my shaking hands would allow.

CHAPTER 12

As soon as I was ready, I grabbed the radio. It slipped out of my clammy hands and fell to the floor. *Nooooo!* I'd just repaired it, and now I'd gone and broken it again. I picked it up and turned it on. Faint static crackled out, and I almost whooped aloud. After forty-eight hours of silence, the static was as welcome as the monsoon rain after drought. The fall must have fixed it, and I couldn't wait to find Dad and tell him that I'd repaired the radio after all.

I clipped the radio on to my belt and did a victory dance. Finally, something was going my way. I picked up my flashlight and tiptoed to the window. An almost full moon hovered in a cloudless sky.

Dorje's coat lay on my bed. I didn't want to wear it, but it was the warmest thing around. I put it on. Outside, there was no sign of Dorje or anyone else. Before my courage deserted me, I climbed out the window and dropped down. My ankles juddered with the impact, and I swallowed a moan.

The forest was noisy with chatters and squeaks. I tried not to imagine the number of rats milling around. The smell of roasted meat and vegetables hung in the air. There was also that underlying ammonia smell. Rat feces.

I thought of Anjali and what she might be doing at camp. Was she still mad at me? Or would she be the tiniest bit worried that Dad and I hadn't checked in for a while? I went with the latter. When this was all over, I was going to apologize and make it up to her. Now, with the radio working, we had a chance!

Dad had mentioned that the ceremony was in a temple in the forest. But there was forest all around us. Where would I start looking? I hurried toward the bamboo grove sure I'd find a clue about where to go next. A few rats scurried by, paws scrabbling in the frozen dirt. Long tails flicked out of sight when I aimed the flashlight at them. It would have been useful to understand what they were saying. What did rats talk about, anyway?

I had to admit that Dad was right: Imdur was an unusual village with its beliefs, rules, language, and deep affinity for rats. It was sure to fascinate the world. But right now, I cared more about getting back home than educating the world about an eco-friendly but hidden village.

The cacophony at the grove intensified. Embers glowed in the firepits, which held the remnants of a feast. Hundreds of rats swarmed around empty lengths of blackened bamboo on the ground, nibbling on the leftovers.

The urge to run back to the guest house was over-whelming. I forced myself to move forward. Leaves rustled overhead, and I flicked the light upward.

Flibbertigibbet.

The bamboo was crawling with black bodies. Red eyes stared at me. If they jumped, they could take me down. Rats were carnivores and cannibals. When food supply was low, a mother rat would not hesitate to snack on her babies. But the villagers fed them well — hopefully they were too full to sample me.

I backed away from under the grove, my fist jammed into my mouth. *Don't jump. Please don't jump.*

Not taking my eyes off them, I popped a candy into my mouth, chewed, and swallowed, almost choking. The sweet-ness helped a little. Four left. I knew I'd better stop, or I wouldn't have any for when I needed them most. If we couldn't contact camp, we'd have a three-day trek through the forest to Leh.

I pulled the radio off my belt and turned it on again. It crackled, a bit louder this time.

"Krish to Adventure Camp," I whispered. "We need help. Do you hear me?"

Static.

Once again, I turned the dial to the frequency Anjali and I had used when we camped with our families. I prayed she'd have a radio with her, tuned to the bandwidth we'd always used. She was smart, and I was counting on her to do what I would do if the roles were reversed.

"Anjali, if you can hear me, please send help. We're in a small village near the Ladakh Range. It's called Imdur. The approximate coordinates are 36 degrees north and 78 degrees east, but it's not marked on a map. Send someone to get us, *please.*"

More static. I thought I heard garbled voices, but that could have been my imagination and a desperate longing to hear a friendly voice. Just in case, I repeated the message twice. I turned down the volume but kept the radio on, too afraid it would die on me again if I switched it off. Till I heard an acknowledgement, the radio would stay on.

What now? There was no sign of the Imdura, the secret ceremony, or Dad. Should I carry on or turn back?

A song wafted up on a chill breeze from beyond the bamboo grove. So that's where the temple was. I could go around the grove, but it would take too long. The forest was full of rats, too, so there was no reason for a detour. Straight through was the best and fastest option. The sooner I found Dad, the sooner we could head to higher ground for a stronger signal.

Imma's voice rose above the rest, punctuated by a series of thumps.

I shuffled forward, flicking my flashlight up and ahead. The air was thick with the musky smell of fur and pee. I was halfway across the grove when a large black rat bounced off my shoulder and toppled down the front of my coat, scrabbling for purchase.

I suppressed a yelp as I flung it away. It fell to the ground, squeaking madly. I crashed through the tall bamboo, hoping I wouldn't squish a rat.

The radio crackled suddenly, spewing garbled words. I thought I heard Anjali say my name. Had she got my message and the coordinates? I held the radio above my head. It knocked against a branch, and a rat scampered down my arm. I cursed and flicked it away. The radio fell silent again.

Fribble!

I was feeling so filthy and wretched, I would gladly have stepped under the icy waterfall if it were close by. The chanting grew louder as I squeezed through thick bushes and bamboo, looking for Dad. Rats swarmed on the path behind me, almost as if they were herding me onward.

The ground sloped away, and I stopped. Below me, in the ravine, was a temple of crumbling stone. Its main platform stood high above the ground, surrounded by four pillars at its corners. Thick vines had a stranglehold on the pillars. A dome jutted from the foliage, as if gasping for air.

A giant deity, carved from white stone, stood in the center of the temple. I could only see the lower half, but the legs and tail were a dead giveaway. It was a rat: what else? A fire burned, bathing the deity in warm, yellow light. Only thirty villagers were gathered around it; this was obviously a private gathering, and we had no business being here. I shivered at the thought of being caught.

Imma and Shalva stood on each side of the deity. Imma was in white and Shalva in black. Night and day, yin and yang, devil and angel. I tried to get my GF to shut up, but it kept screaming *RUN* in an endless loop.

Tashi stood beside Imma in a white robe with a head-dress of flowers and a necklace of white beads. A young boy knelt before Imma, flanked by, I guessed, his parents. He was dressed in a white tunic and pants, with no coat despite the chill.

I crept down the slope carefully, staying low to the ground. The smell around me was nauseating: a mix of rotting leaves, damp earth, and ammonia, which I tried to ignore. Tashi started to sing in a sweet, clear voice. I didn't understand a word, though it sounded nice. I searched the darkness for Dad but saw no sign of him. I stayed out of sight too. The tree cover around the temple was scant, and I was careful not to get too close.

The bitter smell of burning herbs tickled my nose, and I willed myself not to sneeze as I watched with horror and fascination. Imma approached the young boy and raised him to his feet. She was barely an inch taller than him. The boy stood there, head bent and shivering. I felt sorry for him. The least they could do was give him a proper coat. I snuggled into Dorje's coat, glad for its warmth.

"Are you ready to become a man?" asked Imma.

"Yes," said the boy. His voice trembled.

The thumps of the villagers' staffs echoed around the temple like rolling thunder.

"Will you promise to look after your brothers and sisters, to keep the secret of Imdur as long as you live?" Imma stepped closer.

Another secret, I thought with a sense of foreboding. No wonder Dad was right at home here with his secretive mission. The next minute, I was mad at myself. Hadn't I kept the incident with Anjali a secret from our parents? I'd been too ashamed to admit that I had been a coward, and Anjali hadn't said anything either. No one knew why we had gone from being favorite cousins and best friends to not wanting to spend time together.

The villagers thumped their staffs again. My heartbeat raced and tripped over itself.

"Yes," the boy said, taking a step back.

Imma grabbed his shoulder and tilted his chin upward. "And you promise never to betray the Imdura? You accept the consequences of leaving this village?"

"No!" yelled the boy suddenly, shoving Imma's hand away. "I want to leave and go to the city! I want you to let me go without punishment!"

There was that word again. It seemed everyone was afraid of punishment. What were they afraid of? I looked at Tashi; her pale face was scrunched up. Perhaps she was struggling with loyalty to her mother and wanting to leave, just like this scrawny boy. She must feel so trapped.

The boy's father leaped to his feet, his face ugly, arm raised as if to slap the boy. Imma shook her head, and the man dropped his hand. For a small person, she wielded a lot of respect and power.

Imma stepped closer and whispered something in the boy's ear. He nodded. She wiped away his tears and kissed his forehead. And then she did something totally bizarre.

Imma grabbed a fistful of the boy's hair and pulled his head back. She lowered her face and bit his neck. The boy screamed and dropped to the ground, blood trickling from the puncture wounds on his scrawny neck. He twitched violently and was still.

I clapped my grimy hands on my mouth to stop a yell. I'd just witnessed a murder!

Imma signaled to Tashi, who looked at the boy, wide-eyed. She shook her head.

"Do it," Imma commanded. "Now."

Tashi was so pale, she was almost translucent. She shook her head again.

"You have to earn your place as next shaman," Imma said. "*Do it.*"

Tashi dropped to all fours, leaned forward, and bit the boy. Then she raised her head and looked at Imma. Her lips and teeth were stained bright red. The poor boy lay still, his face white as marble.

My GF went berserk: heartburn flared, as if fanned by a strong wind; acid ate through my stomach, turning it to mush.

We'd landed in a village of cannibals. It was definitely time to clock out.

I started to back away, quietly, when the radio squawked to life. This time the voice was very clear and unexpectedly loud.

"Krish, this is Anjali! Got your message. Hang in there, we're coming!"

CHAPTER 13

I'd been desperate for the radio to work, and now that it did, I was horrified. The Imdura turned toward me as one. I almost passed out at the sight of those red eyes staring up at me.

"It must be our nosy guests," Imma said in a low, furious voice. "Find them and bring them to me."

I leaped to my feet. I thought I heard Dad's voice yelling my name, but my head was empty of all thoughts except one — *RUN*. I crashed through the bushes like a crazed elephant. I had to escape from this village, the dead boy, and the cannibalistic mother-daughter duo.

I didn't get far before I had to stop and throw up in the bushes — a hot, stinking mess of undigested dinner. Rats suddenly appeared and swarmed over it. The stink of vomit, mingled with the dank smell of fur, made me sicker. I hunched on the ground, barfing my guts out, unable to get the image of the boy out of my head.

I clambered to my feet and turned to go.

"AAAARGHHH!" My voice echoed through the still night.

Tashi stood in front of me. Moonlight glinted off her pale skin, making her lips appear redder. I would have fallen into the puddle of vomit if she hadn't grabbed the front of my coat to steady me.

"Please don't bite me," I whimpered.

Tashi plucked a leaf from a nearby bush and held it out. "Wipe your mouth. Imma wants to see you."

"Please let us go," I said. "I didn't see a child being murdered, honest. We'll never say a word if you let us go, I promise. You have my promise and Dad's!" My mouth had developed verbal diarrhea and wouldn't stop.

"If you hadn't spied on our sacred ceremony, there might have been a chance," she said sadly. "Did I not tell you that we live by the rules? That you had to stay indoors?"

"Where's Dad? Have you seen him?"

"So, he's spying on us too?" she said, her tone suddenly harsh. "Don't you two have any respect for our wishes? Come on, we can't keep Imma waiting."

As we trudged back to the temple, I berated myself silently. Why had I kept the radio on? Why hadn't I switched it off and tried it when we were in the guest house or the forest?

The thought of being trapped here, and the punishment, made my legs shaky. I stumbled again, and Tashi steadied me, not making eye contact. She was mad at me, and I didn't blame her.

I followed Tashi to the temple. As the Imdura parted to let me pass, they started to chant. Softly at first and then louder, thumping their staffs on the stone floor, glaring at me with red eyes. Their conjunctivitis was worse, and I hoped Dad and I weren't infected. I almost laughed aloud. Pink eye was the least of our troubles right now.

My throat was dry, and my tongue tasted like spoiled milk. The Imdura followed me with their eyes. A few scratched me with sharp fingernails, drawing blood.

"Watch it!" I said, my mind screaming *infection*.

No one apologized. They continued to chant. A few were drooling. Were they rabid?

Where was Dad? I needed to see him so badly.

Imma and Shalva knelt, cleaning the dead boy's face and throat with a cloth. I stared at the parents, who looked calmly at their dead son. They should be raising a stink or calling the police. But they looked proud and happy.

Imma's eyes flicked to me. She looked disappointed, and, somehow, that made me feel worse. It was bizarre.

"Krish!" Dad, hanging on to Dorje, limped up from the opposite direction. I ran to him and buried my face in his filthy clothing. I didn't care about anything except that we were both alive.

"What happened to your foot?" I asked.

"I twisted my ankle when I ran down the slope. It hurts a lot, but never mind me. I thought I heard Anjali's voice on the radio. It's working, right?"

I glared at him, but it was too late.

Dorje held out a filthy hand. "Give me the radio."

I shook my head.

"You have no choice."

"You can't do this!" I said. "Dad, say something!"

"You heard Krish," said Dad through gritted teeth. "It's our property, and we're not giving it to you." He was turning gray and sounding weaker by the second.

Dorje's stern face was unchanged.

I held out the radio, and he snatched it from me. It felt as if I'd handed over my last candy *and* my hand sanitizer.

Imma stood up. Her lips were as red as Tashi's. Her eyes flashed redder. I edged closer to Dad and clenched my fists. No one was taking a bite out of either of us. I would fight them with everything I had.

"Why did you both disobey my orders when I asked you to stay in the guest house?" Imma said in a soft, menacing voice. "I asked Dorje to make sure you were safe before he joined us."

"Safe?" I said, my voice high. "From being bitten by rats or bitten by you, just like you killed this poor bo—" I glanced down. My words dried up.

The boy opened his eyes. He was alive, but now the whites of his eyes were a deep red — as if he had conjunctivitis too. I watched him, ready to leap out of the way if he came for my jugular.

The boy sat up and scrubbed his nose. He sniffed the air. With a joyful whoop, he raced on all fours around the perimeter of the temple. A horde of rats raced alongside him, chittering and squeaking. He stopped in front of the rat deity, kissed its feet, and sat cross-legged. Shalva smeared him with a white paste across the forehead, down his arms, across his chest. Even his legs. Though I knew what came next, I shuddered.

The black rats swarmed all over the boy. He sat still. A few rats clambered over his face, licking off the paste. When it was gone, the rats slipped away. The boy came back to his parents, full of energy and grinning. Except for the conjunctivitis that seemed to be spreading through the village, the boy looked healthy and normal.

"You were saying?" said Imma, her voice chillier than the winds sweeping down the Himalayas.

"I don't understand," I said. "Why did you bite him?"

"It is not your business to see this, let alone understand it," she snapped. "*You* found our village because you were lost. *You* begged for shelter. We could have turned you away to face the forest, the cold, and hunger. Instead, we let you stay. We would have sent you back with a guide, if you had respected our rules. But obviously that is too much to ask of the great photographer Kabir Roy and his sneaky son, Krish. You have repaid our trust with deceit."

My shoulders slumped. Imma was right. We'd abused her hospitality, and we were in the wrong. But how could I sympathize with her and fear her at the same time?

"And you will let us go," said Dad. His face was the color of cement. "Now that the camp knows we're alive, they'll send a search party if we do not respond. I need the radio." His face spasmed with pain, and he moaned.

"Take them back to the guest house, Dorje," said Imma, dismissing us with a wave of her hand. "I will come to take a look at that foot soon." She turned to the villagers. "One more Imdura joins the ranks. Go home and rejoice."

The villagers thumped their staffs one last time and slipped away into the moonlit forest. One of them turned and looked at me, eyes glowing bright. He reminded me of the rats in the bamboo grove a short while ago. An awful thought struck me as I recalled the bitten boy, and Dorje. Surely they weren't … No, they couldn't be. It was just my imagination going wild with the stress of the last few days and suggesting the impossible.

Dorje supported Dad. Tashi walked alongside me.

"Why did you bite that boy, and why did his eyes turn red?" I had to know, and I had to hear it from Tashi.

"Silence!" barked Dorje.

He needn't have worried. Tashi wasn't speaking to me. She wasn't even looking at me.

Back in the guest house, I helped Dad sit down and eased the shoe off his right foot. He groaned, sweat trickling down his white face. It scared me. He was always the one in charge. The groaning, moaning, and sweating were my job!

His foot looked like a large ripe plum. "This looks bad. Dorje, I need my radio, now. We have to call for help to get us to a hospital. Please!" I stared at him, hoping he'd relent.

Dorje beckoned to Tashi, and they both stepped outside, shutting the door behind them. The soft click sounded ominous, as if nothing we said would make a difference. I turned on Dad.

"You *had* to go spy on them when they told us not to! I begged you to stay here. Now look at the mess we're in. What if they don't let us leave? Worse, what if they decide to punish us like they did that other person who threw a boulder?" I was so angry, I was shaking.

"Krish, come here," said Dad softly.

I glared at him. "Why?"

"I'm scared too. But you cannot let fear rule your life."

"Fear keeps you safe and stops you from doing stupid things!" I yelled. "For once you could have listened to me. Especially when I told you it came from Tashi. You already had what you needed. Why did you have to get greedy and ruin everything?"

"We'll get through this," said Dad, looking aghast at my outburst. "I promise."

"You also promised we're leaving tomorrow," I said. "That's not happening. We're stuck here, and we might die here. I thought that if I was more like Anjali, you'd love me like you love her, and listen to me. I was wrong! This trip was a mistake, and I wish I'd never suggested it. You'll never be proud of me, and frankly, I don't care anymore."

Dad lay still, his foot elevated by the camera case. He reached out a hand to me, looking ashamed and sorry. I stayed where I was. Seconds turned into minutes. The fire crackled in the stove. Outside, the soft murmurs of Dorje and Tashi continued.

Finally, Dad dropped his hand and closed his eyes, his breathing ragged. Something inside my chest shifted, hardened. Dad was out of commission. If I lost my nerve, we'd be trapped here for the winter.

It was up to me to get us out of this mess, and this time Dad was going to listen to me, whether he liked it or not.

CHAPTER 14

Imma stepped into the guest house, still dressed in her ceremonial outfit, silver catching and winking in the lamp-light. She smelled of herbs, dank fur, and blood.

Dorje leaned against the wall, and Tashi stood by the door, arms crossed. She refused to meet my eyes. Panic threatened to drown me. I couldn't lose the only ally I had. Somehow, I had to win her back to my side.

"You have disrespected us and abused our hospitality," said Imma, her lips tinged with dried blood. "You spied on a sacred ceremony and took pictures when you were forbidden. Are you always such rude guests?" Imma was a law unto herself, and we'd have to be very careful not to anger her more.

Dad sat up, his face ashen but determined. "I am sorry for disobeying your orders, Imma. But you have such an unusual way of life, I had to document it. If you allow me to share it with the world, they can learn from you and your ways. They can appreciate what you have created, and this will help you too."

"*No!*" Her voice was like the crack of a whip. "We have worked hard to stay away from the eyes of the world, and you will not take that away from us."

"I will pay you for the photographs," said Dad. "I have connections within the government. They will provide the necessary infrastructure: electricity, running water, sewage system, paved roads —"

Imma's lips pulled back in a snarl, revealing razor-sharp incisors. Dad shut up in a hurry. She thrust her face into his and bared her teeth. Tashi tried to grab her, but Imma shoved her away.

"The government, help us?" she growled, her eyes blazing. "They are the reason we're here. The government did not help us when rats destroyed our crops and our children were starving. The government sent us rotten food, and our weakest died a painful death."

Dad leaned back till he was almost horizontal on the cot. "I — I don't understand."

"All you need to understand now, Mr. Roy, is that you are never leaving. You have seen too much, and you lie as easily as you breathe. You cannot be trusted, that is clear to me now. Make yourselves comfortable, because you are here to stay."

The world started to blacken around the edges. I swayed on my feet.

"Krish is going to faint," Dad yelled. "Help him!"

Warm hands clasped my shoulders. "Be brave," Tashi whispered in my ear. Those two small words gave me strength. She hadn't given up on me. The blackness faded. Taking deep breaths, I forced myself to stay upright. I tried to meet her eyes, but she was looking at Imma.

"I know how to make this right, to apologize for my mistake," said Dad. He unbuttoned his jacket with trembling hands.

Knowing how much it was costing him to do this, my throat closed up. If only he'd respected their rules and listened to my warning, we'd be planning the trip back home right now.

Dad took out the Quik-Pik camera and remote and held them out. "You can destroy it if you like. There are no copies."

Imma took only the camera and handed it to Dorje. "Smash it."

Tashi was right. Under that sweet exterior was a will of iron.

Dorje dropped the camera. It bounced on the mud floor and came to rest at his feet. Watching us, he brought his heel down hard, cracking it open. Dad's face was wracked with pain, and I wanted to hug him, but there was one last thing I had to try before it was too late. I watched and waited for my chance.

"Let's look at your leg," said Imma. "Help me, Dorje."

Dorje bent over to help Dad straighten out his foot. The radio was still hanging from Dorje's belt. I grabbed it and sprinted out of the guest house. The plan was to run far enough that I could contact Anjali before anyone caught up with me. I had to tell her we were in danger. They needed to hurry.

Outside, I tripped and landed on something soft. The light from the open doorway illuminated black rats covering every inch of ground around the guest house. They leaped on me — one, ten, fifty, a hundred.

"Get off!" I screamed, batting at them with my arms, trying to brush them off. "Get off me." It was like trying to brush off water during a downpour.

The stink of ammonia filled my nose, and their sharp claws raked my skin as they clambered up to my face, chittering excitedly. Touching those hairy bodies made me want to barf, but if I didn't throw them off, they'd smother me.

A rat scooted across my mouth. Screaming, I jumped up only to fall over again. The rats swarmed over me — a tidal wave of hair, claws, and teeth. That's when I heard an odd sound.

Laughter.

Someone was laughing while I was losing my mind. I curled up into a ball on the ground and sobbed, my eyes shut tight, feeling helpless. I tried to think of anything but being covered in rats. It was impossible. Their shrill cries burrowed into my head like a drill through concrete.

At the sound of clicking, the tide of rats receded. A warm hand grasped mine and pulled me to a seated position. "Don't try to run again. These rats won't let you."

I opened my eyes. Tashi wiped away my tears. "Come back in." Her look warned me not to say anything. This time, I did exactly as she asked, and retrieved the radio.

Dorje stood in the doorway, grinning. How could I have ever believed he was nice? I wished we had walked away that night instead of begging to stay.

I didn't bother with a candy. Even a hundred of them couldn't calm me after this ordeal.

CHAPTER 15

Dorje plucked the radio from my hand as I passed him, threw it on the floor, and smashed it. Radio parts scattered throughout the room. It felt as if he'd stomped on my chest.

"If you cannot follow rules, we have to help you follow them," said Dorje in a polite voice.

Something inside me snapped, and I forgot Tashi's warning. "I don't *care* about your stupid rules and secrets! I just want to get out of here with my dad. You have no right to keep us here."

Dorje looked livid. He spoke to Imma in a series of clicks. Imma clicked back. They were planning something bad, and I looked to Tashi for translation. Her frightened eyes, darting between Imma and Dorje, gave me enough of a clue. Fear thrummed inside me like an electric current.

Dad moaned, and Imma knelt beside the bed, probing Dad's foot with her fingertips.

"The bone is fractured," said Imma. "I will have to bring

the swelling down and then bind it up. Dorje, get a cold compress, warm water, and a clean cloth."

Dorje nodded and left the hut, leaving the door ajar. The rats scampered out of the way, opening a path for him. They moved back as soon as he passed. The rats relied on the villagers for their food and roamed freely. They were trained like dogs to obey the commands of the Imdura, who could, evidently, speak their language. It was a useful skill when there were so many of them. I sat beside Dad, wracking my brains for an escape plan. I was drawing a blank and feeling more panicked with each passing second.

"I have already given you the camera," said Dad in a faint voice. "We have no more pictures. You can search if you like. What more will it take to let us go?"

"I cannot let you leave, but I won't make you suffer while you are here," said Imma. "If that wound is not treated immediately, infection will set in. You could lose that leg or die in severe pain. I have delivered babies and amputated limbs with just herbs from the forest and a couple of strong villagers. Lie back and let me take care of it."

Despite her desire to help, I remained angry at Imma. To keep us here against our will was criminal. I was sure of it. But Imma did not care about laws. We were trapped.

Dorje returned a short while later with a leather sleeve filled with icy water that he made me hold, a cup of green paste that smelled of fresh-cut grass, a bowl of warm water, and clean strips of cloth. Imma wiped the dirt and blood off Dad's leg where the skin had broken. She slathered on the green paste and wrapped the leather sleeve around it. Dad gripped my hand so tight I thought the bones would shatter. I hated to watch, but I couldn't look away from his swollen foot or the toes that looked like grapes.

"This will bring down the swelling," said Imma finally. "I'll put a cast around it tomorrow to help with the healing. Do not put any weight on that foot, or you'll never walk normally again."

Truth or lie?

Dad nodded, wiping sweat from his face with a shaky hand. His eyes had sunk deep into their sockets. He looked twenty years older than when he'd left the guest house a few hours ago.

Tashi hung back after Imma and Dorje walked out, taking all the rest of Dad's equipment and cameras. The look she gave me could have been either a warning or encouragement. Before I could decipher it, Imma returned and dragged Tashi away. The door shut, but not before I saw the ground was still seething with rats. Their chittering had almost become white noise.

I fell back on the bed and stared at the sloped bamboo ceiling. A sliver of pink light outlined the shuttered window.

We'd been up all night thanks to Dad's photography expedition, which had turned into a complete disaster.

"You were right, Krish. I'm sorry I didn't listen to your warnings and your gut feels. Can you forgive me, please?"

I looked at Dad's swollen foot, his haggard expression. I closed my eyes and took a deep breath. *Now* he believed in my GF, when escape was almost impossible.

"Rest, Dad. I'll figure something out."

I JERKED AWAKE. SUNLIGHT seeped in from the window slats. Last night's events flooded my head, and I glanced over at Dad's bed. It was empty.

"Dad!" I leaped up and fell onto the floor, my feet tangled in the blanket. "*Where are you?!*"

The door opened, and Tashi entered with a tray of food. "Why are you yelling?

"Dad's missing," I said, trying to untangle myself from the sheets. "Where is he?" My mouth was dry, and my heart pounded as if I'd run a marathon.

Tashi put the tray on the table and helped me up. "Calm down. Dorje came early this morning to bring him to our home. You were fast asleep, and your father didn't want to wake you. It's past noon now, and you'd better get up."

"Is your mother going to cut off his leg or kill him?" I blurted out, hugging myself tight to stop the trembling.

"She's trying to heal his leg," said Tashi, looking annoyed. "Stop being dramatic."

"The hospital in Leh would have been better."

"Get dressed," she said. "I have to take you to Imma."

"I wish Dorje had sent us away," I snapped.

"If he had, you would both be dead by now," Tashi said, opening the window. An icy breeze wafted in.

"Can you stop talking in riddles and explain?" I faced her. "I have a wild theory, but I want to hear it from you."

"First eat, and then we'll go see your dad." Tashi looked tired this morning, and black circles stood out prominently below her eyes.

I realized I was starving. I sat on the bed and devoured the steamed buns. My gaze fell on the remnants of the radio. I looked away and drank some butter tea. There had to be another way to contact camp, and I was going to find it.

"Can you tell me anything about Imdur?" I said. "That initiation ceremony last night. Why did you bite that young boy?"

"It's a long story," she said, her back to me as she gazed out the window.

"Thanks to your mother, we're not going anywhere any-time soon. I managed to get word out to camp last night. Now all we can do is wait. We have time."

"No, you don't." She turned around and gave me a stern

look. "You barely have any time left. Get dressed. I'll wait outside."

Even though my hands were numb and icy, I dressed in record time. I threw on the rat-fur coat, not giving it a second thought, and grabbed my backpack. It contained my sketchbook and colored pencils, plus the duct tape, the hand sanitizer, and a few odds and ends. It made me feel prepared. Sort of. As soon as I was done, I called out to Tashi to come back in.

"Tashi, are Dad and I going to die?" I asked, just as were leaving.

She froze, not looking at me. I closed the door. This was the first time we were alone after last night's fiasco. I might never get another chance to talk to her without someone eavesdropping.

"Tashi, I know I can trust you to tell the truth. Why aren't we allowed to leave? What was going on last night in that temple? Why did your mother bite a child, and why did his parents not call the police? And why did *you* bite him? Are you *cannibals*?" The questions spilled out without pause.

I took a deep breath and slipped a hand into my pocket to count the candies. There were four left. I let them stay there.

"Imma has forbidden me to say anything," said Tashi. "She knows you're trying to get me to talk." Her eyes were wide with fear.

"I know you don't agree with Imma or Dorje." I was going out on a limb here, pitting daughter against mother, but I had to try. My GF encouraged me. "What Imma is doing, forcing us to stay, is criminal. She's forcing you to be shaman, to follow the rules even though you don't like it. Right?"

"We're not criminals!" she said, glaring at me. "Why should I help you when you have such a low opinion of us? When you insult me and my mother with every breath you take?"

"I'm sorry!" I said. "I didn't mean it like that. You're generous, and you gave us food and shelter. But we need to go back home. How can Imma not understand that? Doesn't family mean anything to her?"

"I will come for you at midnight," said Tashi. "You have one chance to escape before the full moon feast, the day after tomorrow. I'm only doing this so you don't think too badly of us. We want to be left alone, but your dad's pictures would have put us all in danger. If you tell anyone about us or lead them here, you could still kill us all. I don't know if I'm doing the right thing." She took a deep breath and opened the door. "We have to go, or Imma will send someone to look for us."

"You are doing the right thing, Tashi. You are! Thank you."

Suddenly, Tashi dropped to the ground and pounced. She stood up clutching a small rat in her hand.

"Why are you here?" she hissed. "Who sent you?"

The rat squealed and twisted in her hand, trying to bite her. Tashi bit its nose, drawing blood. The rat shrieked.

Tashi flung the rat away, and it landed on its feet. "Don't you dare spy on me again!" This was followed by a series of clicks that sounded a lot like curses.

Was Tashi yelling at a rat or a person?

My GF, helpful as ever, supplied the correct answer.

CHAPTER 16

Imma's hut was as gloomy as before, and more fragrant. But this time there was an underlying tinge of something foul — like rotting garbage on a summer's day. Was Dad dead and decomposing? I shook my head to get the horrible thought out. I slipped off my boots at the door and raced inside.

"*Dad!*"

Imma appeared from the back of the house, wiping her hands on a rag. She smiled. "Good afternoon, Krish. Sleep well?"

"Where is my father?" I asked, my eyes riveted to the smears of blood on the rag.

"I took care of him," said Imma, holding my gaze. Cold hands wrapped around my heart.

"What do you mean?"

"He won't be in pain anymore." She refused to give me a straight answer, seeming to enjoy my panic.

I understood that she was protective of her people, her

village, and her beloved rat ancestors, but this was just mean, playing with me when she knew I was worried and scared. I raced past her into the backroom, bracing myself. If she'd hurt Dad, I would make her pay.

The room had a crackling fire and was warm and cozy. Four beds were placed along the walls, and only one was occupied. I rushed over to Dad, who lay still. His face was corpse-gray, and a stink of sweat and pee hung over him like a cloud. He didn't move or open his eyes. His bandaged foot was back to normal size, though blood blossomed around the ankle where he'd twisted or fractured it.

"Dad!" I yelled, sticking a finger under his nose. He was still breathing. I sat back, dizzy with relief. I would gladly listen to his lectures about my phobias if only he'd wake up and talk to me again.

"He'll be sleeping for a few hours," said Imma. I started and whirled around. No surprise that I'd not heard her enter. "But he's fine now, and the foot will heal normally as long as he doesn't put any weight on it for at least a month."

"We're leaving as soon as Dad wakes up, whether you like it or not." I glared at her, refusing to give her the satisfaction of seeing how close I was to bawling.

Imma gripped my hand and pulled me out of the room. Her sharp fingernails bit into my skin. Tashi, who'd been cleaning up the living room, stopped and stared at us.

"Tashi, our guest is a little overexcited. Make him some tea and add the calming herbs. You like those, don't you, Krish? You said they took away your anxiety."

I wanted to tell her to go jump off a cliff but swallowed the words. Playing along with her would be the smarter thing to do. Tashi had promised to help, and that calmed me.

"Sure," I said, deciding to throw the tea away when they weren't looking. I needed a clear head, and the anxiety would make me careful. I remembered how I'd cuddled the rat the last time I'd had tea with Imma. She wasn't tricking me into doing weird stuff again.

"You're a fast learner," she said. "Make it now, Tashi, and take a cup to Shalva, too. He's not well and is resting in his room."

"Yes, Imma," said Tashi, giving me a warning look before she walked away.

I was going to be on my best behaviour. She needn't have worried about me.

"Come with me, Krish," Imma said. "I want to show you something."

Imma tied her hair in a loose bun and threw on a black fur coat. She bowed her head in front of the altar by the door. It was a clay figurine of a white rat about as tall as my knee — their deity. I tried not to think of the boy's red eyes after the ceremony at the temple. I tried not to think of anything other than what I needed to do to get out of Imdur.

Outside, the late afternoon sun had turned the snow-capped mountains to gold. A few villagers went about their work. Birds chirped overhead. The smell of woodsmoke and food wafted by as we walked past the bamboo huts.

"Learn to appreciate the now, Krish. Imdur has no cars, no traffic, no stress. Just nature and peace all around. How can you not love it?" Imma sighed deeply. "Every day that I wake up in this paradise, I thank Shubra-Musa for guiding us here. But we'll be moving soon." She looked at me, wanting me to ask the obvious question.

"Where are you going?"

She pointed to a mountain, slightly taller than the rest, with a somewhat flat top. "There are many caves in that one. We've been preparing for months now. After the feast and before winter arrives, the Imdura will leave this village and move into the caves. They're sheltered, and there's zero chance of travelers stumbling upon us. We will be safe there. You and your father are our last, but permanent, guests."

I said nothing, but my brain scurried in my head like a trapped rat.

Imma patted my head, almost fondly. "I like you a lot, Krish. Your soul is pure, and if you stay with us, it will remain pure. Unfortunately, I cannot say the same about your father.

His soul has been corrupted by greed. He disrespects us. He was taking pictures even at the purification ceremony, wasn't he?" Her gray eyes locked with mine.

My GF tingled. She had guessed the truth, and we were prisoners here, so what was the point in denying it?

"Dad didn't mean any harm, and you already destroyed his camera, and took all the others. Even if we said anything after we left, who would believe us without evidence?"

Imma fixed her gaze on me. "I cannot trust your father now. With or without pictures. He might still lead people back to us. We've faced death too often to take the risk again. No, you will both stay here, Krish. You might as well get used to the idea."

Breakfast started to climb my throat again. I'd not felt like barfing this often anywhere else on this trip. The worst part of it was, it would not be wasted. Gross.

A rat with dried blood on his nose chittered at our feet. A cube of ice skated down my spine as I realized it was the one Tashi had bitten. Imma stopped and looked down, listening intently. It was telling her something — but what?

Imma clicked back, then looked at me with narrowed eyes. She stroked my cheeks, sharp nails scraping my skin intentionally. "Go back to my house and drink some tea. You will feel calmer. I have a few things to attend to."

She strolled away, greeting villagers along the way.

Tashi stood in the doorway of Imma's hut.

"Did you see what just happened?" I asked.

She nodded.

"Who was that rat?"

"My brother, Norbu," she said. "He told Imma you asked for my help to escape. She's keeping an eye on us both from now on, and getting away will be a lot harder."

It felt like the time I'd missed a step walking into the basement. Except this time, I was tumbling down a steep flight of steps without end.

I was almost sure I knew Imdur's secret.

CHAPTER 17

"You'll still help me?" I said as calmly as I could manage. "Even though your mother knows?"

"Yes," she said, her eyes meeting mine. I saw courage there and felt slightly better. If she could be brave about going against her mother, so could I.

While Tashi made the tea, I watched her. How could I have thought I was the superior one just because I came from the city and went to a fancy school? Dad's life and mine were in her hands, and I hoped she would come through. The risk was huge, and I still couldn't get that scream out of my mind after Dorje had sent rats to punish the person who'd thrown the boulder. I shuddered and tucked my hands into my armpits to stop them from shaking.

As soon as Tashi was done, we carried the cups into the living room. There were so many questions buzzing in my head, I didn't know where to start.

"Are there any more travelers in the village?" I asked as soon as she returned from taking a cup of tea to Shalva.

"Anyone hidden that we should know about?" There was safety in numbers, and if there were others, we might have a better chance of standing up to the Imdura.

Tashi gave me a dirty look. "No. I've told you before, we don't like travelers here, nor is our village easy to find. We get rid of them as soon as we can. You have stayed the longest, and if Imma has her way, you will not be leaving."

Her words chilled me, and I had to make sure she was firmly on my side.

"I want to show you something," I said, pulling my sketch-book out of my backpack. "You'd asked what the city was like. Take a look."

I handed it to her, explaining each scene as she flipped the pages: home, school, the library, a busy street, and the Taj Mahal. She traced a fingertip over the pictures, her face bent low.

"What's the Taj Mahal?" she asked. There was curiosity and wonder on her face, and for the first time she looked and sounded like a teen, not someone preparing to become shaman of a village.

"A monument of love that the Mughal Emperor Shah Jahan built for his wife, Mumtaz Mahal, after she died. It's one of the most beautiful structures in the world. We saw it on a school trip, but I've been there a couple more times with Mom and Dad."

"I wish I could see it too," she said wistfully. A teardrop plopped onto the page. She sniffed and wiped her face. "I've been to Leh with Imma. I want to see what I'm missing — what we gave up to keep our secret from the world." Her voice was soft, but her eyes reflected the anger she felt at Imma's ironclad rules.

"You can come with us, you know."

"I can't …" Her voice trailed away. "I dare not."

"If you're unhappy or in danger, you have to leave," I said. "You can stay with us: Mom, Dad, and me. Think of us like your family. Whenever you want to come back, we'll get you back here safely." I had no idea what Mom would say if we brought back a strange girl with us, but I felt sorry for her. Clearly, she did not want to be the next shaman. And someone in the forest was out to get her. Child services would never force her to stay in a situation where she felt unsafe or where she was forced to do things against her will.

"So, what do you say?" I prodded gently. "Are you brave enough to leave and follow your dream?"

Tashi took a gulp of tea. She flipped through the rest of the sketchbook, her eyes lingering over each image. She saw the ones I'd made of her and blushed.

"Krish," Dad called out just then. I raced into his room, Tashi right behind me. Dad looked like he was going to die in the next few minutes. His face was gray, and his eyes had sunk so deep into their sockets, they almost seemed hollow. The stubble made his skin look even paler.

"How are you feeling?" I asked, sitting beside him.

"Terrible," said Dad. "What time is it?"

"Four in the afternoon," I said, glancing at my watch.

"Did Imma change her mind, will she let us go?" he asked, trying to sit up. He fell back moaning, his face glistening with sweat.

"No, but Tashi has agreed to help us escape. Right?"

Tashi held out a small cloth pouch, her eyes darting to the doorway. "Hide it quickly. Imma will be here any minute. Try to avoid eating any of the food Dorje brings. But if you must, mix this powder in your food before you eat. It will counteract the herbs they're adding to make you sleep."

"Your mother wouldn't —" I started to say.

"Yes, she will," said Tashi, cutting me off. "She and Dorje talked about this last night. We — they — cannot risk you trying to run away."

I liked that she'd corrected herself. She was definitely on our side, and I was relieved.

"Your only chance of getting away is to stay awake tonight. I'll show you where to go, and you make a run for it tomorrow night, before the day of the feast. After that, we're all moving to the caves Imma showed you."

She stopped abruptly and cocked her head to one side. I

couldn't hear a thing, but I knew enough to trust *her* hearing. With strength that belied her thin frame, Tashi hauled me to my feet and raced for the living room, pulling me along. We sat down just as the door opened and Imma came in.

Tashi calmly sipped her tea. I did the same, wrapping my hands around the cold clay cup, trying to keep them from shaking.

Imma walked into the sickroom. "How is your leg?" she asked Dad. The curtain swished closed, and the voices became faint. Dad murmured something too soft to hear. I wished I had Tashi's hearing. Imma returned seconds later, still talking to Dad. "I'll give you something for the pain. You will spend the night here so I can keep an eye on you, Mr. Roy."

No! I wanted Dad back with me so we could plan our escape.

Tashi saw my face and shook her head.

"Why don't you take Krish back to the guest house," said Imma. "We have a lot of work to do, for the feast and our move to the caves. I'm sure he'll amuse himself and not do anything stupid." Her gray eyes skewered me, waiting for a protest.

"Yes, Imma," I said and went to say bye to Dad. As I leaned forward to hug him, I whispered in his ear, "I have a plan. Don't worry."

"I should have listened to you sooner, Krish. I'm sorry." He clasped my hand tight, his eyes searching mine. "I'm so sorry."

"You're listening now," I said. "That's enough."

Tashi walked me to the guest house. "Midnight. Don't eat the food Dorje brings, no matter how hungry you are. Or, if you're too hungry, mix the powder first."

"I'll be ready, and I'll try not to eat anything."

She was playing with the tassels on her coat, twisting them around her fingers.

"We'll be okay," I said. "You'll love Delhi, and you can start going to a proper school."

She shook her head. "Don't be too sure. My brother, Norbu, is a sneak, and he's jealous of me. He wanted to be shaman, but I have the gift. He'll do anything to make me look bad."

I didn't want her to back out or have second thoughts. It was selfish of me, but she was our only chance. "We'll be very careful." On an impulse, I hugged her. She was so rigid, I wondered if I'd made a mistake being so familiar with a future shaman. Just as I was about to draw away, she patted my back awkwardly.

"May the blessings of Shubra-Musa be upon us," she said when we drew apart.

"The white rat you guys pray to?" I asked. "What's the deal

with that?" I still hadn't figured out how that fit into their weird secret.

"I'll explain later," said Tashi, eyes darting, ears twitching. "I have to go."

"I'll take any blessings, rat or otherwise. See you tonight."

CHAPTER 18

At midnight, I was ready and waiting.

Though starving, I hadn't touched the food Dorje had brought earlier that evening, even with the powder to counteract its effects. The sounds of chatter and the smell of roasting meat wafted in through the open door as he set the tray on the table. From the window, I saw fires blazing, throwing up red sparks like confetti. I hated the Imdura for being so happy when I had been in constant panic mode these last few days.

Luckily, Dorje had dropped the food and left, sure that I wouldn't wade through the puddle of rats around the guest house after my meltdown the last time. But Dorje hadn't counted on Tashi helping me.

I had waited till Dorje was out of sight and thrown the food to the rats outside. They pounced on it with delighted squeaks. It was fascinating and revolting to watch them. Moments later, they went still, toes curled, mouths open. I ate three of the remaining candies to stop the rumbling in my stomach. I would save the last one to celebrate our escape back to Leh.

I paced the room, agonizing about all the things that could go wrong, until Tashi tiptoed in after the lightest tap on the door. She was dressed in black from head to toe, a black scarf covering her hair and face so that only her eyes showed. She carried a sharp spear.

Tashi led me through the back door and into the forest. A nearly full moon bathed everything in a silvery glow. The forest was awake. The deeper we went, the louder the squeaking and chittering grew. I stumbled often, and Tashi reached out to steady me. She, on the other hand, was sure-footed and quiet.

The rats kept pace, scurrying along the branches from tree to tree. Leaves rustled, twigs snapped. An overpowering stink of rat lingered in the air.

Tashi clicked in annoyance.

"You can *all* talk to the rats?" I asked.

"Only those in whom the gift is strong," she said. "Especially the shaman. Now shhh ... it's not safe even to whisper."

"How much further?" I asked, pressing a stitch in my side.

Suddenly Tashi squeezed my hand and pulled me into the bushes. "Quiet," she whispered. "Don't move."

A shadow flickered not too far from where we crouched.

"Who is that?" I whispered, wiping sweat from my burning eyes.

"A rogue villager," said Tashi.

"Is he dangerous?" I asked.

"Shhhhh!"

Too late. Someone reached into the bushes and hauled us out. A tall man dressed in furs, stinking of pungent BO, glared at us. His black hair was slicked back and shiny. I reached for Tashi's hand.

"Namaste, Shaman Junior," said the man, displaying yellow teeth, sharpened to points. "Imma is slipping up if she lets you wander around in the night or get caught by me."

Tashi stood tall, though her hand trembled in mine. "Let us go, Rinchen, or you'll be very sorry."

"Who is this?" Rinchen said, glaring at me. "Another poor traveler Imma is trying to dupe? The way she duped us, chaining us to the village with her miserable curse?" Rinchen edged closer, his breath so foul, I tried not to breathe at all. "If I had her neck in my hands right —"

"She did it to protect us," said Tashi, cutting him off. "It may not be what everyone wants, but it's what most of us want."

"She ruined our lives!" Rinchen said. "No one should be forced to stay if they don't want to, gift or no gift. We're stuck!"

"Is that why someone threw the rock at me?" She sounded furious, and I remembered the incident in the forest yesterday. And what happened after.

"Dorje took care of that, didn't he?" said Rinchen. He whipped a blade from his belt and held it at Tashi's throat. "I should pay him and your mother back in kind, right now."

Tashi laughed. "Go ahead and do what you want. The village and its safety come above all, even me."

"What's he talking about?" I asked, looking from Rinchen to Tashi. "What gift, what curse?"

"Haven't you told this boy what Imma has in store for him?" Rinchen said, pacing in front of us. "He deserves to know the truth."

A volley of clicks and squeaks shot out of Tashi's mouth.

"Should we make a run for it?" I whispered.

"Wait," she commanded.

Suddenly, a wave of rats slid down from the tall bamboos around us and launched themselves at Rinchen. Within seconds, they were dropping on him, teeth bared, claws ripping into his clothes. As quickly as he brushed them off, more arrived, squeaking excitedly.

"*Run!*" yelled Rinchen as he raced away, rats still clinging to him.

And suddenly I recognized his voice. It was like plugging a finger into an electrical socket. *This* was the voice I'd heard on the mountaintop just before we descended into the valley. He'd warned me to run even then.

I took a few deep breaths, but it didn't help much.

Footle.

Flannel.

Flapdoodle.

My T-shirt stuck to my back. I shrugged off the coat and draped it on my arm. Hanging there, it looked like a giant rat, which was worse, so I put it back on.

"Hurry, we're close," said Tashi. "And forget about Rinchen. He's a troublemaker."

"You still haven't told me why he can't leave Imdur. Or you. Why are you stuck?"

We crested a hill, and below me a river glistened silver in the moonlight. "Canoes!" I said, forgetting all about grilling Tashi for answers. "So that's how you get to Leh in a hurry. Dorje lied to me." My pulse raced, and my stomach heaved. Escape was right here in front of me, but it meant getting into the water. How was I going to manage that when I couldn't swim even to save a life?

Tashi nodded. "That is the Indus River. It is two hours to Leh by canoe."

I slid down the hill on my butt, not trusting myself to walk down in the semi-darkness without tripping. Tashi uttered a few squeaks. A dozen rats poured out of burrows and holes in the riverbank and spread out in the forest.

"These ones are my friends," said Tashi, watching my face. "They'll keep an eye out for us against Imma's spies or Norbu, who is sure to come looking for me. Let me show you how to use the canoe. I know you have questions, and I'll explain everything on the way back."

The riverbank was thick with poop. My eyes watered, and I held my hand over my mouth and nose, counting back from a thousand. I glanced around as we hurried toward a rough pier, making a mental note of the landmarks. A Himalayan birch, shaped like a fan, stood beside the pier. On the opposite side of the river was a mountain with a top shaped like an arrowhead. It would guide Dad and me when we had to make it here on our own, tomorrow night. That is, if Tashi couldn't leave without raising suspicion.

Two canoes were tethered to wooden posts at the end of the pier. They were small but sturdy. Oars lay inside each one. The canoes pointed downstream, ropes taut in the swift current. They looked like straining dogs on a leash. I thought of Anjali thrashing around in the water. How was I going to do this? I couldn't.

Except, this was the only way out.

Tashi pulled a canoe toward us and tightened the rope

so that it lay alongside the pier. She jumped in nimbly and looked up at me. "Now you try," she said.

The river charged by like a rhino. Somewhere in the distance, I was sure I heard the roar of a waterfall or white water. My brain froze. I couldn't do this. I slipped my hand in my pocket for the last candy. My fingers closed around it. Not yet.

"Jump!" Tashi said.

I fought to stay calm. My hands were cold and clammy, while the rest of me was on fire.

"We don't have all night," said Tashi. "Jump, Krish. I'm here to help you."

I threw off my coat, jumped, smacked my stomach on the edge of the canoe, and fell into the water. Icy needles slid into every part of my body. I thrashed and swallowed water as I sank. This would be a fitting end for a coward like me. I'd not saved Anjali from drowning, and this was how I would die.

Tashi's strong hands grabbed hold of me and held my head above water. When I had calmed down somewhat, she helped me climb into the canoe. She watched me as I sneezed and shivered.

"Again!" she said. "Your lives depend on it. If you can't get in on the first try, you'll be caught. You won't get another chance when the whole village is chasing you."

"I can't!" I said, coughing up water. My body shook as if I had flu. "I'm not cut out for this kind of adventure stuff. That's Dad's territory."

Tashi grabbed the front of my sweater and pulled me close. Her lips were drawn back in a snarl. "Do you want to go home?"

I nodded.

"If you think you can't do it, you won't. If you believe you can, you will."

"Let me go!" I snapped, tired of being lectured by Dad, Imma, and now Tashi. "I told you, this is too hard for me."

"All right," said Tashi, pushing me away. "Norbu will be here any minute. He's always keeping an eye on me, and he'll report back to Imma." Her eyes swept the riverbank. "It'll be over soon. Welcome to our family." She stood up and reached for the pier, ready to haul herself up.

Suddenly, Anjali's voice was in my head. *You can do this, Krish. I know you can.* I had to see her again and ask for her forgiveness. The only way that would happen is if Dad and I escaped, using these canoes. I stared at the river. It was only water, after all. I could do this. I was *going* to do this, or I would never be able to look myself in the mirror.

"You're right, Tashi," I said, taking in a deep breath and meeting her eyes. "I'll do this till I get it right. I have to."

She rewarded me with one of her rare smiles.

I fell in a few more times, but I kept going. By the eighth try, my teeth were chattering so hard I could barely speak. As I sat on the pier, a rat raced up my leg and chittered back, watching me expectantly. "I'm not talking to you," I said, flinging it into the water. "I'm just cold."

It swam to shore, fighting the current all the way. I'd read that rats were good swimmers, but to swim against the current showed me just how strong they were. Within a minute it was on the opposite shore. I saw its red eyes catch the moonlight and then it was gone. Indestructible. No wonder the Imdura worshipped them.

"We don't have much time, Krish," said Tashi quietly. There was desperation in her voice. I had to try harder.

On my eleventh attempt, I landed in the canoe without tipping it. Jubilantly, I looked at Tashi, and she gave me another smile. We headed back up the slope, away from the stiff breeze. In the shelter of the trees, I caught my breath.

"Thank you," I said to Tashi as I slipped into the warm and dry coat. She had been right to insist I keep it. Despite the gross factor, it was a lifesaver.

"Tomorrow, leave shortly after midnight," said Tashi. "If you are still here the day after tomorrow, it'll be too late."

"Too late for what?" I asked. "Are you going to tell me everything now, or are we still playing twenty questions?"

Tashi stopped and looked at me. She seemed to be glowing

in the light of the moon. "Imma will make you an Imdura," she said. "Once you become like us, there's no leaving even if you get the chance to escape."

The boy's initiation ceremony flashed through my head. "She'll bite me and Dad," I said, a wave of dizziness crashing over me.

"Not your dad, just you."

CHAPTER 19

The weight of Tashi's words made my knees buckle. I sat down. A couple of inquisitive rats climbed into my lap, and I shot to my feet, sweeping them off.

"What will she do to Dad?"

"If you hadn't disobeyed the rules, she would have let you go," said Tashi. "A few travelers have come and gone. Most have felt the need to photograph Imdur, just like your dad, then lie about it. Imma never forgives liars, nor does she let them go. Did you not see the wall of souvenirs in our house?"

I remembered the items in detail: the lone ski and goggles, the backpack, the copy of *The Lion, the Witch, and the Wardrobe*. And a pair of glasses on a silver chain. Those people were still here, in spirit. A chill seeped into my gut.

"Why bother to heal Dad's foot if she's going to kill him anyway?" It was hard to think those words, let alone say them. I shivered as if I had a bad case of the flu.

"Imma doesn't like to see anyone suffer," said Tashi,

sniffing and twitching. "Our ancestors have suffered enough. But she will not tolerate disobedience or a threat to the village. Your father is guilty of both."

"Tell me everything, now!" I was sick to my stomach with what I had seen so far and what my GF was telling me. But I had to know the truth, no matter how impossible or scary.

"Our ancestors came from Mizoram a hundred and fifty years ago," said Tashi, pacing in front of me. "They had wheat and rice fields surrounded by bamboo forests. They lived in peace and comfort. Every forty-eight years, the bamboo flowered and gave fruit. The earliest incident recorded by our ancestors was in 1815, and the second one in 1863 which is when they decided to move. The bamboo fruit attracted insects and vermin. Especially rats. They came in the hundreds to eat the fruit. Because there was so much food, they multiplied rapidly. There were thousands within a few weeks. But once the fruit was gone, the hungry rats turned to the crops to feed themselves and their young. Within days, they ate the grain and destroyed all the fields. Our ancestors were starving, but there was no help from the government." She was silent for a few seconds, watching me.

"Go on," I said, though shivers were starting to wrack my body. I desperately needed dry clothes, but I needed to hear the end of this story even more. Rats the size of kittens scurried around, setting my teeth on edge. I grabbed a stick and thwacked it on the ground, earning a frown from Tashi.

"Somehow, our ancestors managed to survive the 1815 attack," said Tashi, scratching her nose, twitching restlessly as she rubbed her hands together. "Forty-eight years later, it happened again. The moment the bamboo started flowering, the villagers pleaded with the government for help. They warned the government about the rat attack, but no one took them seriously. The rats arrived and destroyed the crops yet again. When there was no more food, they sneaked into houses and dragged away newborns. It was a very bad time for everyone. Finally, the food trucks arrived." Tashi's voice wobbled. She hugged herself tight as if to steady herself.

The horror of it made me want to sob too. "So, that's good, right?" I whispered, though my GF told me there was worse to come.

Tashi shook her head. "The food was mouldy. But everyone was so hungry, they ate it. The young and old were the first to go. They died painfully, vomiting till the very end. Parents saw their children suffer an agonizing death. No one ate any more of the poisonous grain, but they were still starving. Desperate, they started eating the only thing in abundance."

She stopped pacing and stared at me. "Do you understand what I'm saying?"

"They ate the only thing in abundan—" Suddenly, I knew. "Rats! Your ancestors ate rats."

She nodded.

I quashed the bilious tide in my throat. "People around the world eat lots of weird things — frogs, cats, dogs, even cockroaches and crickets. The main thing is, they survived that horrible time. Right?"

"We didn't just eat them, we prayed to the gods to become them. Rats are intelligent and strong. They adapt to any situation. And that is what we needed. To adapt, survive, and live."

"You're talking in riddles, Tashi, and you said we don't have much time."

"Imma's great-great-great-grandmother was pregnant during the rat attack in 1863. She was starving, and her baby was in danger. She caught a rare white rat and ate it raw. Somehow, she and her baby survived. The baby — a girl — was born pure white, just like Imma and me. The villagers discovered she was strong — a fighter and survivor. Our ancestors built Imdur and learned to be self-sufficient and this albino girl became Imdur's first shaman. We stay hidden, keeping to ourselves and not letting anyone know our secret."

"Eating rats is hardly a secret worth keeping," I said, annoyed with the long-drawn-out explanation about something so common. "People in China, Indonesia, Cambodia, and Vietnam eat them. They don't keep it a secret. It's not a big deal."

"But this is," said Tashi as she threw off her coat.

Her skin sprouted fur, and a long pink tail snaked out behind her. Her fingers grew longer, ending in sharp nails. Finally, her nose elongated into a snout, sniffing the air. Her ears twitched. Still human-sized, she dropped to all fours and crept toward me.

My heart almost stopped as she came closer. It was the stuff of nightmares.

I closed my eyes and forced myself to breathe. How would I ever see Tashi as a human again? How would I ever forget the fact that she was an extra-large rat?

I breathed in. I breathed out.

When I opened my eyes, Tashi had changed back into human form. Her eyes pleaded with mine as she shrugged into her rat-fur coat. They asked a silent question, but I had no answer.

"You're all like that?"

She nodded.

"And you can change to any size?"

"Small and large, as the situation demands."

I massaged my temples. This was huge. Too huge for my brain to wrap around.

"The shaman bites twelve-year-olds in a coming-of-age ceremony," Tashi continued, now talking rapidly. "It makes them transform faster, and they're able to help around the village when we're cut off from the rest of the world. Being a rat gives us the strength to survive in these harsh surroundings. We need nothing and no one else — especially the government. You see why Imma was so angry when your father suggested getting help from them? We don't trust them anymore."

"But how did this happen?" I asked. "People around the world eat rats, but no one has heard of this type of bizarre change. Surely your ancestor eating a rat couldn't result in this. I just can't believe it." I kept my distance, unable to bear standing close to her.

"We don't know for sure, but it had a lot to do with faith and a desperate will to survive," said Tashi. "The story passed on from one generation to the next is this: the child born to my ancestor who ate the white rat was strong. As she grew older, she started exhibiting signs of the change: excellent hearing, a keen sense of smell, and super-intelligence. As the story goes, a snake was hiding in the roof of a house, ready to strike an unsuspecting victim. She sensed the danger, changed into a rat, and killed the snake before it could strike. Over time, the white rat, Shubra-Musa, became our god."

My thoughts were so scrambled, I could barely string two words together in reply. Any biologist would give a kidney to study an Imdura. Immediately, I was ashamed. How could I even think that way? I was proving Imma's theory right. If outsiders knew about them, they would have no peace, no life. They would become lab rats, literally.

"This is why your mother does not like travelers — so no one knows you can transform into rats."

"Every shaman must protect her people at any cost. Imma will do everything in her power to keep us all safe. Call us weird, but it helps us stay alive, and that's all we want — to be left alone to live our lives."

"How did the rest of the people change?" I asked.

"Over the years, our ancestors figured out that a bite from a rat-human helped others to transform," said Tashi. "So, every child undergoes the initiation ceremony at age twelve. Like the one you saw."

"Where does Rinchen fit in to all of this? Why is he roaming the forest and attacking you instead of staying safe in the village?"

Tashi glanced around and lowered her voice so that I had to lean close to hear her even though it made me queasy. "Imma is the most powerful of all shamans to date. She put a curse in place so that anyone who stepped beyond the boundaries of Imdur or tried to leave without permission would turn into a rat. And a rat they would stay till they returned to Imdur. It was to preserve our secret and keep the rest of us safe."

I shook my head. This was so bizarre, it sounded like the truth. No one could have that good an imagination. I was at a loss for words.

Suddenly, a small, wiry rat jumped onto Tashi's shoulder and bit her ear. She yelped and threw it off. As soon as it landed on the ground, it transformed. Norbu stood there, glaring at her. "You are in big trouble, dear sister. They are coming."

Tashi wiped her bleeding ear and glared at her brother. "Always following me around, like a sneak. You're more a dog than a rat. Shoo!"

"*I* should have been shaman," he said, glaring at her. "You have no pride or loyalty."

"Only the power," she said, grinning nastily at him. "I will banish you from the village when I become shaman. I promise you that."

"Wait till I tell Imma what you've done, then we'll see who stays and who goes."

Brother and sister circled each other. Any minute they might rip each other's throats out. If Norbu won, I would be in deep trouble.

Tashi glanced at me. "I can hold him if you want to run. Get into the canoe and go. It's two hours to Leh if you follow the river. *Run!*"

I couldn't abandon Dad even though he'd lied to me all this while and ignored my every warning. He was still my dad, and I loved him.

"I'm not leaving without Dad."

Norbu grinned. "You can't, even if you want to."

Tashi slapped him. He laughed and danced out of reach.

A group of Imdura, led by Dorje, quietly surrounded us. This time I saw them for what they really were. Rat people.

"Tashi, what have you done?" said Dorje, shaking his head. "You, our next shaman and protector."

"Krish is innocent," she said, her voice strong. "We have to let him and his father go."

"That is for Imma to decide," said Dorje. "Let's go back."

A few Imdura fell into line behind us, herding us toward the village. Norbu had disappeared, probably racing ahead to report to Imma. What would happen when she found out that I knew their secret? I glanced at Tashi, but in my mind I saw a large rat walking upright.

I stumbled, and Tashi grabbed my hand to steady me, just as she had before. Instinctively, I snatched it away. Her transformation played in my head like a bad song on an endless loop. She was a filthy rat and crawling with germs. They all were.

Tashi looked so hurt that she drew away from me, her body rigid. A sudden thought struck me: is this how Anjali had felt when I'd run away? I was filled with shame and horror.

I wanted to reach out for Tashi's hand, but mine seemed to be frozen. I couldn't do it.

"Krish, listen to me," Tashi whispered as we walked. "It's important."

"Okay," I said, focusing on putting one foot ahead of the other.

"I could never have left Imdur, but it was nice to dream that I could," she said. "You can still get away if you keep your nerve, and, as promised, I will help, even though you can't bear to be near me now."

I was drowning in shame, though my skin crawled every time I imagined her in rat form, creeping up to me, sniffing at me. She was trying to help, and I was being a total weirdo about it.

"I'm sorry I'm this way," I said. "Germs scare me. Never liked rats much."

She stared at me like she wanted to say something. She opened her mouth and closed it again. Our fragile friendship had shattered.

Dorje marched us back at a fast clip. Imma and Shalva were waiting for us outside their home, surrounded by the entire village. Dad had also managed to hobble out. He leaned on a crutch, looking as if he would faint.

The chant grew louder as we approached, ringing out in the cold night, echoing in the valley surrounded by the snow-capped mountains that stood sentinel.

"Taazamaas."

"Taazamaas."

"Taazamaas."

"They keep saying this when they see us. What's it mean, Tashi?"

Looking straight ahead, she replied. "Fresh meat."

CHAPTER 20

Imma's hair rippled in the breeze. She looked as if she were carved from white stone, just like their rat deity, Shubra-Musa.

"He knows?" Imma asked Tashi.

"My sneaky brother already told you, so why ask?" said Tashi. She stood up straight, arms crossed. I envied her calm confidence.

"Why did you betray us to this useless boy?" said Imma. Her voice was soft, but her eyes were glowing coals. The wide-spread conjunctivitis, especially at night, now made sense.

"I am sick of our secret," Tashi replied. "I refuse to do this anymore."

"So, you would rather kill your entire village, sacrifice us all, to save two ungrateful travelers?" said Imma. "I expected the next shaman to show more responsibility and loyalty." Her face displayed contempt.

This was my fault. I was making the same mistakes all over again. I'd failed Anjali when she'd needed me the most.

Now, I'd begged Tashi to help me, and I wasn't even defending her.

"Why take in travelers if we're going to kill them?" said Tashi, marching up to her mother. "How different are we from the government who sent poisonous food to our ancestors? They killed us with kindness, and now we're doing the same."

Dad hobbled up to me and put an arm around my shoulder. "I should have listened to you," he whispered. "These people are horrible."

"Not all of them," I said.

"What secret is Tashi talking about?" asked Dad. "What did she tell you?"

Imma gave him a malevolent look, and I knew she'd heard him. She threw back her head and let out a piercing cry. I clapped my hands to my ears as the villagers answered. As we watched, they changed: elongated snouts, clawed hands, fur and thick pink tails sprouting on their bodies. They surrounded us, clicking their teeth, sniffing, drooling.

Dad squeezed me so tight it hurt. But he kept me on my feet. I did the same for him. We were fresh meat. Only Imma and Tashi stood between us and being eaten alive by human-sized rats.

"So, the rumours I heard were true," Dad said, his voice shaking.

"Yes, but you will never tell anyone," said Imma.

"This will remain a secret," said Dad. "You have my word."

"You had a chance to prove your trustworthiness and failed," said Imma. "Do not waste your time, or mine, by asking again."

I was very close to losing it now that I'd seen all the villagers in their true form.

Floriferousness!

Tashi and Imma faced each other, their hackles up. They reminded me of rams who butt heads to show strength. But Imma had the upper hand. She was still shaman, and the most powerful to date, according to Tashi.

"I will do anything you say if you let them go," said Tashi. "I'll start training to be a shaman tomorrow, and I will act responsibly."

I felt smaller than a tick on a dog. Even though I'd been rude and unkind, she was still putting our safety before her plans to see the city or leave Imdur.

"Life is precious," said Imma. "No one knows better than I. But these two have broken every rule and must be punished."

"But Krish didn't do anyth—" Tashi started to say.

"He knew what his father was doing and did nothing to stop it, nor did he inform us," Imma said. "He is guilty because of his silence."

I hated to admit it, but she was right. I had known about Dad's deceit but had said nothing. I was an accomplice. It was also true that if Dad got away with the pictures, he would sell them to the highest bidder. Once the world found out about the Imdura's transformational abilities, they were doomed to life in a lab. Or worse.

I clung to the hope that Anjali was organizing a rescue. But what if this time she decided to see *me* drown and ignored my plea for help? It would serve me right, and yet I knew she was better than I'd been. She had said they were coming, and she would keep her word.

Display over, the villagers turned back to their human forms. Actual rats still milled around us, chattering and adding to the cacophony.

"Tashi is a traitor and has no right to be our next shaman," one of villagers said. "She should be sacrificed to Shubra-Musa and another chosen in her place."

Many shouted their agreement.

"I'm loyal, am I not, Imma?" Norbu said. "Shouldn't I get the chance to be shaman?"

Tashi threw a venomous look at her brother. The muttering swelled. The Imdura inched closer, their breaths a white cloud above their heads as the moon hovered like a spotlight over the macabre scene.

I had to act. Now.

"No!" I said, stepping closer to the villagers. "Tashi will make an excellent shaman. She cares about people, and she will care about you all. I forced her to tell me your secret — this is all my fault." There, I had done it, and though I was petrified, a part of me felt good.

"Krish, shut up!" Dad yelled. "Are you mad?"

I ignored him and spoke directly to Imma. "Please give Tashi another chance."

Shalva shuffled forward, and the Imdura fell silent. His eyes cleared, like the sun coming out from behind a cloud. "I am with this young traveler," he said in hoarse voice. "Everyone deserves a second chance, and we Imdura are forgiving, if nothing else."

Imma rubbed her eyes and sighed. "It's almost morning. We will discuss this tonight. In the meantime, get some rest and be ready to move to the caves after the feast tomorrow." She sniffed the air. "Snow is coming, and we don't have much time. Dorje, take Kabir back to the guest house. Tashi and Krish, you will come inside with me."

"I'd like to stay with my son, please," said Dad.

"You do not deserve even the courtesy of a reply," said Imma. "But I will say one thing: you have ruined hospitality at Imdur for every traveler after you. Because of your deceit, it will be hard to trust any stranger from now on."

Every word was a hammer blow because it was true. Dad

looked shamefaced, but how would that help now?

"Dad, I'll be okay. Get that weight off your foot and relax," I said calmly, though my GF was working overtime wondering what new torture awaited me in Imma's home.

"Be careful, Krish," Dad said, looking like he was about to faint.

He limped away with Dorje. Tashi and I followed Imma. I forced myself to touch Tashi lightly on the shoulder. It was a small first step.

"I'm sorry for the way I behaved," I said. "Can you please forgive me?"

She nodded but took care to keep her distance. I didn't blame her. I'd hurt and insulted her.

As we walked inside, past the ghastly souvenirs on the wall, I couldn't help thinking I could have been out of here by now — paddling toward Leh, where I could have raised the alarm to rescue Dad. Had I done the right thing staying back, or had I made the biggest mistake of my life?

The truth was, I couldn't have left him behind, no matter how scared I was. My days of running away were behind me. Of that, I was sure.

Shalva plunked down on a chair by the fire and took up his knitting. One needle was silver and the other black. He gave me such a piercing stare, I felt like a shish kebab. It was as if he knew I was the needle thief.

"Tashi has to be punished," said Imma, pacing the living room, ignoring us both. "What am I going to do with her, Shalva?"

"He said everyone deserves a second chance," I piped up. "Surely you're not going to disrespect him. That would make you a hypocrite."

Imma's furious look made my spine melt. I forced myself to hold her gaze.

"Come," said Imma, pushing me in front of her. "It's time we shut you up." Tashi followed quietly.

Imma stopped in front of a black door. "Inside," she said, opening it.

"May I please have a lantern?" I was scared of the dark, but I wasn't going to admit it to her.

"No," said Imma, smiling coldly. "You can sit in the dark and think about all the ways you've made this worse for yourself."

I clung to the doorframe, pleading with her mutely. Imma dug her nails into my arms. As soon as I let go, she shoved me into the room. I staggered in and hit my head on the wall. Before I could recover or turn around, she'd pulled the door shut. There was only the faintest bit of light seeping in from a tiny crack in the roof.

"Help!" I pounded the door. "Let me out."

"Why are you torturing him?" I heard Tashi yell. "You're cruel and heartless and I hate you!"

"In order to protect your loved ones, you have to be cruel," Imma said. "The next time you open your mouth to speak nonsense, you will regret it! Until I think of a suitable punishment, you'll stay in the house. And if you let Krish out of that room, I will feed him to the rats and make you watch."

I pounded on the door again. "Let me out! Please! I'm very sorry for what Dad did."

Footsteps receded, and there was silence.

I sat on the floor, my back against the door, and hugged myself tight. The almost-darkness was a living thing, smothering me. I couldn't breathe. The world tilted and whirled. Panic made me light-headed.

Breathe.

I thought of Tashi and how brave she'd been even though her mother and the entire village had turned against her.

Breathe.

I thought of Anjali's terrified expression when she'd found herself in deep water with a severe cramp. She managed to stay afloat till help arrived, even though I'd run away.

Breathe.

I'd walked through that mucky riverbank despite the rats and the poop. I'd practised getting into the canoe even though I was terrified of the water. *I* had done that. Me. I wasn't giving myself enough credit. I was so busy arguing about my phobias they'd become permanently mine.

Only I could change me. Starting now.

A part of me still hoped that Dad would come up with a plan. He was always the rescuer and I the rescued. But he was injured, and it was up to me now. Slightly calmer, I glued my ear to the door. Was that Tashi or Imma in the kitchen? I could continue pounding on the door, but I knew it would be useless.

There was a tiny sound behind me. Still on fours, I turned around. Two red eyes floated toward me. Closer, still closer. I could just about make out the shape of a large rat, clicking its teeth.

I fainted.

CHAPTER 21

When I came to, tiny feet were scrambling over my face. It sounded as if the room were overrun with rats, and the stink was overpowering. Their red eyes, which was all I could see clearly, looked like fairy lights scattered across the ground till I remembered that their sharp teeth could rip me to pieces.

I sat up so fast, the room spun. So, this was Imma's punishment. She'd sent in the rats to devour me. By the time I was found, my bones would be stripped clean. I guess that empty spot on the wall was where my skull would hang.

A pair of red eyes scurried closer. My breath came in ragged gasps as I hugged my knees tight and covered my face. As soon as the first rat made a move, the others would pounce. I was going to die in the filthiest, most painful way possible: being eaten alive. I stuffed a fist in my mouth to stop from screaming.

If I'd ignored those rats in the forest, we might be free. We might be back home. Follow the rats, I'd told Dad. Where there are rats, there are people and food. There'd been food, all right, and it had walked into the village on its own feet.

I jumped to my feet and paced, too wound up to sit still. I made up my mind to wring a few necks, stomp on a few rats before they devoured me. I was not going down without a fight!

"Come on then!" I whispered, bouncing on the balls of my feet. "Come and get me. I'm not scared of you lot! Okay?"

A pair of red eyes inched closer. Others followed. My vision blurred, and I was finding it harder to breathe the foul air. I forced myself to remain standing. I heard a soft plop as a rat jumped onto my boot and clambered up my leg. I swept it off with such force, it smacked against the wall with a dull thud.

A crescendo of squeaks filled the room as the rats rushed to their fallen friend.

"Anyone else want a taste of that?" I yelled. "You lay a paw on me and I'll squish you like a grape." I stamped my feet to show I meant business. Scores of red eyes were bunched up in a corner as if the rats were holding a meeting.

Go on, I thought. *Discuss what this monster will do to you if you come close.* I hopped in place, not taking my eyes off of them.

They seemed to have finished their discussion because they all faced me, resembling a row of Christmas lights lying on the ground. One of them gave a piercing squeak followed by a series of short clicks.

"Shut up!" I yelled. "You don't scare me."

They retreated into a corner, and the sound of scrabbling and scratching filled the tiny room.

Suddenly, I could see them clearly thanks to a strip of light under the door. There were close to fifty rats in the room. If they decided to jump me all together, they could take me down. My bravado melted. Who was I kidding? One bite and I would get an infection, chills, fever, and die an agonizing death.

I sank to the floor and sobbed as the scratching became more frenzied.

A slithering sound caught my attention, and I jumped to my feet. A thin bamboo stake slid under the door. Tashi was giving me a weapon to defend myself. *Yessss!* I snatched up the bamboo and knelt toward the sliver of light to examine it. One end was sharpened to a point.

"Thank you, Tashi!" I whispered, in case Imma or Shalva were close by.

I grasped the bamboo and crawled toward the largest rat. It stood watch while the others continued to scratch away at a corner of the packed mud floor. Kill the leader and the soldiers will scatter. Classic battle strategy. The rat must have sensed something was wrong. It stood up on his hind legs and squeaked frantically.

"Scared, are you?" I said, clasping the bamboo in my sweaty hands. "See this point? It's going straight through your heart. And then the rest of you are next." My eyes swept the others, who'd stopped scrabbling. A sea of red pinpoints stared at me.

I prodded the large rat's chest. It pressed itself against the wall and squeaked. In my head, it sounded like, "Help." *Focus, Krish*. This was no time to imagine a hungry rat as the star of *Ratatouille*. This wasn't a Disney movie. I was fighting for my life and freedom.

The large rat dropped on all fours and nudged my stick to one side. *What the —?*

I swung it back and poked harder. The rat froze and looked at me, not attempting to save itself or run away. This was odd. All I had to do was apply a little more pressure and the stake would go right through its heart. I'd give it a good twist. Then let's see how brave the others were. We locked eyes.

I couldn't do it.

Though my brain insisted I go through with the plan, my hands wouldn't obey. I couldn't skewer a defenseless animal, even to save my own life.

I dropped the bamboo stick and grasped my head. I was an idiot. The rat nudged the stick with its nose, pointing toward a spot in the corner where the other rats were busy. They were trying to tell me something, and, finally, I understood.

There was a tiny hole through which I could see sunlight. They were digging an escape route and wanted my help.

"Move aside!" I said, getting to my feet.

The rats parted, and I started digging as fast as I could. The rats pushed the mud and dirt out of the way so that it did not pile up near my feet. The large rat squeaked orders like a general. I stopped after ten minutes of furious activity. The hole was considerably larger, but it would take more time for it to be big enough that I could push through. I sat down, breathing in the cold, clean air. Knowing escape was imminent, I was calmer.

The rats took a break too, watching me. General Rat (that's what I called it) ventured close. It ran up my leg and perched on my knee. My first instinct was to sweep it off. I didn't.

It sat there, trembling.

I sat there, trembling.

It was scared, but it had come up to me anyway. I stroked its back. The fur was smooth. It squeaked softly, and I took it as encouragement. I had to do something nice for it, show General Rat and his army that I was grateful. I had only one thing to give.

I took the last candy out of my pocket, unwrapped it, and offered it to General Rat. It sniffed the candy and, with a happy squeak, scurried off to show the prize to the others.

"Thank you," I said softly. "Thank you all." I was sure these were Tashi's friends. She'd sent them to help me because she couldn't.

I stopped digging when I heard Imma's voice outside the door. Tashi was arguing loudly, warning me to stop what-ever I was doing. I shoved the bamboo stake in a corner and covered it with rags. The rats raced out of the hole and blocked the late afternoon light.

When the door opened, I was sitting with my back to the hole. Imma stood outside while Tashi came forward and put down a plate of food. Her face was tear-stained, but her eyes shone.

"How is Dad?" I asked.

"Eat," Imma answered. "And do not talk to my daughter."

"I want to see him."

"You will see him at the feast tomorrow," Imma replied.

"Your secret is safe with us," I said. "Because we owe our silence to Tashi, not to you."

Imma shook her head. "See, that is the problem with secrets. The moment one other person knows it, it's not a secret, nor is it safe."

"You said you let some travelers leave," I reminded her. "Why not us?"

"Dorje went to Leh to make inquiries. Your father had been asking about us based on some rumours he'd heard. These could only have come from the family we let go last summer because their child needed a hospital." Imma sighed. "We did the right thing by allowing them to leave. They promised they would keep our village and location a secret, but obviously they talked. You and your father are worse, and trusting you is out of the question."

Her words made sense, and I almost nodded but stopped myself in time. This meant we'd never see Mom again. She would never know what had happened to us. Tears gathered in my eyes, and my throat closed up.

"Once a person has greed in their heart, truth and decency are pushed out," Imma continued. "We cannot trust your father. You are a different matter. You have the qualities of a good Imdura, even though you disappointed me yesterday. I will give you a second chance and allow you to be one of us."

"I'd rather die!"

Imma gave me a sad smile. "If you carry on this way, you might get your wish. Though I hope not. I really do like you, Krish."

She followed Tashi out the door and locked it.

CHAPTER 22

As soon as they left, I jumped to my feet. The rats poured back in. There had not been one squeak while they'd been hiding, and Imma hadn't detected their presence despite her excellent hearing.

We redoubled our efforts, and by the time it was dark outside, the hole in the corner of the hut was fairly large. I kept testing to see if I could squeeze through. For once, I was glad to be scrawny. I'd be out of here sooner, and we'd escape tonight. I refused to let myself think of any other outcome.

The preparation for the feast tomorrow was in full swing. Excited chatter, punctuated with laughter, filled the air. Someone was practising drums, the sounds reverberating through the valley and into my jail room. Also seeping in were smells of roasting meat and boiled rice. I was ravenous despite the meagre meal Tashi had brought a while ago.

As soon as I was free, I'd head straight to the guest house and hide. At midnight, Dad and I would run for the canoe.

I'd have to help Dad, who wasn't comfortable with the crutches. What had taken Tashi and me fifteen minutes would take him an hour at least, maybe more. With any luck, this time tomorrow we'd be in camp.

General Rat nipped my finger, jerking me out of my reverie.

"Aaaaghhh!" I dropped the bamboo stick and stared at my hand. The skin hadn't broken and there was no blood. "What's the idea?" I snapped. "I thought we were friends."

General Rat raced out of the hole and looked back. It dawned on me: the hole was big enough to get through. The rat had realized it before I had.

I was free!

I squeezed out, the rats squeaking encouragement. Halfway through, I was stuck. I thrashed and twisted. Dirt, soil, and bits of bamboo seeped into my mouth. I coughed and choked. Moonlight glinted just beyond reach. I sucked in a lungful of clean air, but I was well and truly stuck. I couldn't move forward or back. Panic ballooned, filling my chest.

"Help!" I said softly.

A rat nipped my bum hard. It was so sudden and painful, I jerked forward and scrambled out. General Rat sat still, waiting for me to figure it out. And I did. The bite had been just the incentive I'd needed to get free.

For a minute, I stared at the rats who'd helped me. Without them, I would still be imprisoned, waiting to become an Imdura.

As I reached for the General, a part of me quivered in revulsion. And yet I wanted to do this. I looked into its black eyes and stroked its back. It squeaked in delight. The rest of the rats clambered all over me. I stood still, breathing deeply, trying not to scream or run.

"Thank you," I whispered. "Thank you all so much."

Tashi hurried out the back door and found me covered in rats. She clicked her tongue. The rats chittered and ran off — a rivulet of black disappearing into the undergrowth.

"We don't have much time," said Tashi.

"Those rats were awesome." I could not believe I was saying that.

"They're loyal to me," said Tashi. "But there are many snitches in the village loyal to my mother. My brother is the worst. He will not hesitate to raise the alarm if he sees you. Stay hidden till it's time to leave."

"Got it," I said, eager to go to Dad.

"Listen carefully," said Tashi. "Imma has gone to the temple to pray. She will be there till sunrise. You must get out after midnight, when most of the villagers will have gone home. I'll meet you in the forest."

"Shalva?" I asked.

"I've already mixed some herbs into his food. He will sleep through the night."

I clasped her hands in mine. Tashi stared at me, confused. "I am so sorry for my stupidity earlier," I said. "Can you please forgive me?"

Tashi smiled and nodded. She pressed a cloth pouch into my hands. "These herbs are for your father, to dull the pain. They're strong, but the effect wears off quickly, so give them to him just before you set out. He will have to make a run for it. The woods are full of Imma's spies and a few more rogues like Rinchen. They'll raise the alarm as soon as they see you. If you're not on the pier by the time Imma gets word, it's over."

"What about his foot?" I asked. "Imma said Dad was not to put any weight on it in case it was fractured."

Tashi shrugged. "The bone will have to be set again, but at least you will be out of here. If you're still here tomorrow, a broken bone will be the least of your worries."

I tried not to think of everything that could go wrong. I was free, and that was a good first step.

"I'll make sure there are no sleeping herbs in your food tonight, and I'll send an extra portion," said Tashi. "Eat well. You will need all your strength to help your father get to the canoe. Run as hard as you can, Krish. This is your last chance."

She'd thought of everything! "You'll make an awesome shaman. I wish you were coming with me."

"I wish I were too, but you hate rats," she said. "You'd hate me too, once I turned into one."

"No!" I said. "But are you sure that will happen? What if this is just a lie spread by your mother to keep you all here?"

"I guess I'll never know, because I'm not leaving," she said. "I know you said that only so I would help you. But that's okay. I want you to go back to your family."

My throat closed up, but it was time for the truth. "Yes, I lied before, but I mean it now. If you want to come with us, you will always be my friend, no matter what form you take. I promise."

Her smile was sweet and sad. "Thank you. I believe you mean that. Now go. Can you find your way back on your own?"

"Yes. Thank you!"

"Thank me when you're on your way to Leh," said Tashi, her voice catching. "Go."

I raced around the back toward the guest house, glad for the cover of darkness. I stopped a short distance away and checked the back door. No one was keeping watch, so I crept in.

Dad was sitting on the cot, head in his hands.

"Dad!"

He tried to stand, but I lunged forward and hugged him.

"What happened?" Dad asked, his eyes wet with tears. "Why are you so filthy?"

"Imma locked me in a room," I said. "Tashi helped me escape. We have to run for it tonight. There's a canoe by the river. If we can get to it, we can be in Leh in a couple of hours."

Dad closed his eyes and took a ragged breath. "I can barely walk. I can't do this, Krish."

I stared at Dad. It was rare to see him talking the way I would have not too long ago.

"Tashi has given me herbs to reduce the pain. It's just a short distance to the canoe, and then we're free. Remember what you told me when we were lost? 'You have to make do with what you have and dig deep when things go south. It's called survival.'"

Dad's eyes glistened. "Look at you, telling me to be strong. I'm proud of you, Krish. Very proud. We'll leave tonight, and I'll take just the camera hidden in my backpack which Dorje missed. It would take an arm and a leg to replace —"

"No," I said, cutting him off. "We're taking nothing that will slow us down. It will be hard enough as it is."

Dad opened his mouth and then shut it. "You're right. How can I be thinking of something so stupid when we're running for our lives and I can barely walk?"

"Let's rest," I said. "We're going to need all our strength."

"I *hate* rats, especially these rat people!" Dad said as he lay down on the cot. "I wish I'd never taken on this assignment and stayed at the camp instead."

I felt like a fraud. One: I was taking my sketchbook, tucked into my pants. It was the only record I would have of Tashi now that we both knew she couldn't come with us. Two: I liked General Rat and its army. Thanks to them, Dad and I still had a fighting chance.

CHAPTER 23

Time crawled by like sleepwalking ants. When Dorje brought dinner for Dad, I made sure I was hiding in the outhouse, my scent masked by something stronger. Everyone expected me to be in Imma's hut, and Dorje could not discover I had escaped.

As soon as he was gone, I raced back in. Dad divided up the food, which I knew was safe because Tashi had sent it. I devoured my share, but Dad picked at his.

"Maybe if I have some of those herbs now, I'll feel hungry enough to eat?" he asked.

"Tashi told me to give them to you just before we start out. They're fast-acting but wear off quickly. We can't spare a single bit right now. Sorry, Dad."

He forced a smile and nodded.

"We'll be fine," I said. "I have faith in Tashi and her herbs. We'll make it to the canoe, and before you know it, we'll be back home, telling Mom this story. How about we get some sleep? Tashi suggested we move after midnight."

"I'm so proud of how you've taken charge, Krish, and enlisted Tashi's help. I wouldn't trade you for a million Anjalis. You're perfect just the way you are, and I'm sorry it took me so long to realize it." He pulled me into a tight hug.

Something in my chest relaxed. "You mean that, Dad?"

"Every single word," Dad replied, looking at me and probably *seeing* me for the first time.

I smiled. My throat was so tight, I couldn't speak.

After dinner, we lay down to rest. So much depended on how quickly Dad could move. Even with no injury, it had been tough for me. With crutches, speed was out of the question. Stealth was out of the question, too. Then there was the water and getting into the canoe. Even though I'd practised it, there was no guarantee I'd be able to do it again. I was dreading every aspect of our dash for freedom. And I didn't have a single candy left to calm me down.

I took a deep breath. No one was going to touch me or my dad. We were going to make it tonight. Dad believed in me. Now *I* had to believe in myself, or this wasn't going to work.

MY WATCH BEEPED SOFTLY in the darkness. I was up immediately. Dad didn't stir.

"Dad! Wake up," I said, shaking him.

He was feverish. Not good. I turned up the lantern wick

and helped him sit. He looked like a corpse being forced to revive.

"Ready for our adventure?" I asked, trying to sound calm.

He grimaced. I realized he was trying to smile. "Bring me a glass of water, please."

Dad took out the pouch of herbs from under his pillow. His hands trembled. I tiptoed to the window and looked out.

"All clear. Dorje's not around." They knew Dad could not get far on his broken foot, and they assumed I was still imprisoned in Imma's hut. They'd let their guard down.

I brought a glass of water over to the cot. Dad opened up the pouch. I shone a flashlight on its contents. The herbs were gray-black. They could just as easily be rat poop, but I trusted Tashi and knew they would help Dad despite how horrible they looked.

Suddenly, Dad sneezed. Powder and water scattered all over the floor.

Furibund!

I dropped on all fours, trying to scoop up the gray-black bits. I only managed to smear them more thoroughly on the mud floor. I sat back on my haunches.

"How much powder fell into the glass?" I asked as calmly as I could. There was no point having a meltdown. I needed all my energy to make sure we could get to the canoe. I

reminded myself that Dad was ill and this was an unfortu-
nate accident. If anything, I should have been more careful
and poured the powder into the glass myself.

"Maybe a quarter of it," he said.

"Drink up and let's go."

"Krish, why don't you go and get help? If I'm still here,
good. If not, at least I will know that you are safe, and your
mother will not be alone. I would never forgive myself if I
slowed you down and we both …" His voice trailed away.
I knew what he meant.

"Would you have left me behind?" I asked.

Though he was pale and exhausted, his look told me that
he got my point.

"Exactly," I said. "We both go, or we both stay."

"Let's do this," said Dad, sounding like his old self.

I helped him up and handed him the bamboo crutches.
The armpits of his jacket were bloodstained.

"It's nothing," said Dad when he saw me looking at them.
"The skin is chafed, and it bled a little. I'm okay now."

He winced as he adjusted the crutches under his arms. He
was lying. If only I had poured the powder into the water
instead of letting Dad do it, he wouldn't be in so much agony.

"Let's go," I said and hurried to the back door.

I opened it, and Dad swung through. A stretch of ground,
free of tree cover, separated the huts from the forest. The

going would be slow, and I would have to keep a sharp look-out for rats — real and human.

Heart pounding, hands clammy, I pointed. "We're heading for the path over there."

Dad's breath came in sharp gasps, and I knew he was already in pain.

Thunk. Slide. Thunk. Slide. Thunk. Slide.

We made our way painstakingly toward tree cover. Each *thunk* slammed my heart. I kept glancing around. No one was following us. A few more steps and we'd be in the forest. I wanted to plant my shoulder into Dad and push him the remainder of the way. Or drag him there. But there was no point rushing him now. He'd have to go much faster once we were discovered.

Fifteen feet. Ten feet. Five feet.

After what felt like forever, we were in the forest. Dad was bathed in sweat and gasping for breath. I had the sense not to tell him this had been the easiest part of the journey.

"Doing great, Dad! Let's move a little faster."

The sound of chittering grew louder. I looked up slowly. Hundreds of rats were perched above us on branches and bamboo stalks, tails snapping like whips. *Friend or foe?* I wondered as I looked into their glowing red eyes, which were everywhere.

Suddenly, they shrieked as one, raising the alarm.

"Go!" I screamed.

We crashed through the trees like a couple of crazed elephants.

CHAPTER 24

I'd lost all sense of direction. None of the landmarks looked familiar. I was only aware of the rats. They kept pace in the tree canopy, their shrieks echoing through the night. Dad hobbled along and stopped every few feet to adjust the crutches and catch his breath.

The drums began, their tempo matching my pounding heart as we raced toward the riverbank. Rats fell on us like fat black drops of rain. They bubbled up from holes in the ground like oil, spreading, trying to hem us in.

A sob escaped me. I was going to die here, in this bizarre village far from home. I would never hug Mom again. I would never read another adventure story in my cozy bed or kiss a girl. And I would never have a chance to apologize to Anjali.

Dad grunted and fell over. He was white and trembling. The bandages on his leg were bright red, and dark stains covered both armpits.

"Almost there," I lied. "Come on, Dad, lean on me. We can do this!"

His weight made my knees buckle. I almost collapsed but forced myself to stay upright and put one foot in front of the other. Sweat poured off me despite the chill in the air. We hobbled through the trees, swatting off the rats raining down on us. They bit us and tumbled away while others tried to swarm up our legs. They were trying to slow us down.

"Where are you, Tashi?" I moaned.

Suddenly a rat landed on my nose. I grabbed it and snarled. "Got you —"

It was a white rat with a red mark near its snout. I gently placed it on the ground, and the rat changed into Tashi. She crouched on the forest floor, ears twitching, eyes sweeping the darkness around us. She looked scary, but beautiful too. "This way," she said.

Dad and I followed her. She clicked her teeth, racing ahead. I hoped General Rat and army would arrive to help us again.

The sound of the drums rolled over us in waves. It was a call to arms, and we were the target. Had any other "fresh meat" made a break for it? Or were we the first?

The squeaking and shrieking grew louder and more

frenzied. Tashi hurried on, taking the easiest route possible, pointing out roots and logs. Without her, we would have been running blind and would have been hopelessly lost. The bright moon was a help and a hindrance. We could see, but we could also be seen.

"How is your leg?" she asked Dad.

He gasped, unable to speak.

"You didn't take the herbs I gave you?" she said, rounding on us.

"Dad sneezed and spilled most of it," I said.

"I should have brought more, but Imma was on her way back, so I ran. Word of your escape has reached her. She is angrier than I have ever seen her. She might not wait till the feast to carry out her plan."

In the clearing up ahead, rats fought each other ferociously. A large black rat who reminded me of the General pounced onto a larger one and bit it.

"This one's Samya, my most trusted friend," said Tashi, not breaking stride. "She'll clear the way for us."

"Was she the one who helped me out?" I said, trying to ignore the stitch in my side and my screaming muscles as I tried to support Dad.

"Yes, and she's the one who led you to Imdur when you were lost in the forest. She's a great fighter and very intelligent. The others listen to her."

So now the bizarre behaviour of those rats made sense.

Suddenly, we heard an agonized squeal. I looked back. General Rat — Samya — was shrieking with pain as ten rats jumped on her.

Tashi sent out a volley of rat-speak, but it was too late. Samya had stopped moving. There was barely anything left of her. I stared, aghast. She'd helped me out and shared my last candy. I couldn't believe the pain I was feeling at the death of a rat.

"Move," said Tashi. "Don't let her death go to waste."

The drumming intensified. Voices yelled out to each other, coming nearer.

"Almost there," said Tashi, still dealing with the rats that launched themselves at us from every direction like furry missiles with sharp claws and teeth.

"Come on, Dad, you can do it."

Dad's face was slick with sweat.

"I can't," he said. "I can't go on any longer. You go, Krish. Save yourself. At least one of us should go back. Leave me."

"I'm not leaving."

Tears cascaded down his cheeks. I was close to losing it too. The rats leaped down, nipping us before falling away. Blood trickled down my face, arms, and legs. I barely noticed. I had to get Dad moving again.

"*Stop!*" Imma's voice echoed around us. All sound ceased, as if the very forest was waiting for her next command.

"Go!" said Tashi.

CHAPTER 25

We ran.

Dad was sobbing and hopping between his crutches, his face a mask of pain. I stayed close, supporting him.

Tashi raced ahead, ducking and weaving and sprinting with ease. The stink of our fear filled my nose, along with the foul smell of the vermin.

"Faster, Dad!" I yelled.

"I'm trying, Krish!" he said, and then stopped suddenly.

He sank to the ground, trembling violently and coughing so hard, I thought his lungs would spill out. "Go," he said. "I'll hold them off as long as I can."

Rats climbed over him, tearing at his clothes. He swatted them away, but they kept coming, wave after wave after wave.

"These are Imma's rats, and they'll keep coming," said Tashi, wringing her hands. "If we don't go now, it'll be too late. Move!"

"Get up, Dad! I'm not leaving you." I tugged at him. "You've always taught me to be strong. To push through the fear. Now you're behaving like a total loser!"

He stared at me, but I was beyond caring. "If you give up, I'm staying here too. Mom will never know what's happened to us. You can do this, Dad!"

Dad leaned forward and pushed himself off the ground, taking all his weight on the uninjured leg. Tashi draped his left arm over her shoulders and I took his right. Both of us took up a crutch each, in our free hands, for when Dad could use them again. Sweat burned my eyes, and my legs were on fire. And still we kept going.

Norbu burst out of the trees in front of us. "Stop, *dear* sister, or I'll rip your throat out."

"Get out of the way, Norbu," said Tashi.

Norbu edged closer, his black eyes flicking between us, a trickle of saliva oozing down his chin. "Imma told me to keep you here while the others catch up. And I will. You'll never be shaman now."

Tashi slipped out from under Dad's arm replacing the crutch for support, and stalked toward Norbu. "Go!" she said under her breath. "I'll take care of this rat."

Though I hated leaving her, I reminded myself they were brother and sister. They wouldn't kill each other, would they?

I gave Dad the other crutch and we hurried on as I tried

to clear a path. I couldn't stop myself from looking back as screams filled the air. Tashi and Norbu had both changed into rats, one black and the other white. They flung themselves at each other, claws out, jaws snapping.

"Almost there, Dad!" I said, trying to convince myself as much as him. "Just a bit further."

Dad hobbled faster, cursing with each breath. Rats poured in from all sides and spread around us — an inkblot staining the ground black. I swung a branch to beat back the rats. It was like trying to fight the sea. Dad needed both hands for the crutches, and he cursed aloud as rats fell from above and hung tight, weighing him down.

We crested the hill. The river, a silver snake in the moonlight, was right there, within reach. A small fire burned on its bank, close to the birch tree. I barely gave it any thought as we hurried downhill. Halfway down, Dad tripped and fell. There was an audible crack. Dad screamed and went quiet.

"Dad!" I yelled, but he was out cold. He'd broken his leg this time for sure. The canoe was so close, but it might as well have been on the moon. I couldn't carry Dad, and I couldn't leave him.

It was over.

Clicks and squeals filled the air as the villagers caught up to us. Their red eyes were fixed on us as they drooled and crept closer.

"I'll kill anyone who touches me or my dad!" I yelled. It was false bravado, and they knew it.

"Make way for Imma!" someone called out, and the crowd parted.

Dad was still out cold. I slapped him. I tried to drag him to the river, but he was so heavy, I couldn't move him an inch. "Please, Dad!" I sobbed. "Wake up."

A hand grabbed my shoulder. I screamed and turned around, brandishing the branch. It was Tashi. Her face was a bloody mess. Blood blossomed from numerous cuts on her hands and legs, but she was here. If I'd had a hand free, I would have hugged her.

"Come on, we'll drag him together," said Tashi. "It's down-hill. No one will touch you while I'm here."

We grasped Dad's arms, and together we pulled him, inch by inch, through the muck and filth toward the canoe.

"Stop!" said a soft voice.

"Keep going," said Tashi. She turned around to face her mother.

"Let them go, Imma," said Tashi.

"When you are the shaman, the fate of the Imdura will rest in your hands," said Imma. "Until then I make the decisions, and I command you to stop them."

"You will have to go through me to get to them," said Tashi, barring the way.

Dad was starting to stir. I slapped his face a few times. He moaned and opened his eyes. "Can you walk?" I whispered, kneeling beside him. "We're almost there. Just a few feet more and we're free."

"I can't get on my feet," said Dad, looking as if he might pass out again. "But I can crawl."

"Okay! Let's go."

Rats scurried down the bank. They edged forward, teeth clicking, sharp nails scrabbling in the dirt as they eyed us hungrily. The Imdura were being held back by Imma. They would take us down the second she gave the command. Only Tashi stood between us. What could one girl do against a village of rat people and their powerful shaman who'd do anything to keep her secret safe?

Dad started to crawl, slowly, painfully, toward the canoe at the end of the pier. I walked beside him, urging him on, keeping an eye on the rats behind me. I'd snagged one of Dad's crutches earlier and I smashed at the rats as they crept close. If only Anjali could see me right now. Clothes and hands filthy, knee-deep in vermin, cleaving a path to freedom.

Two hundred feet.

"Tashi, you still have a chance to stop them," said Imma calmly. "I don't want to hurt you, but I will if I have no choice."

Imma probably thought she could bully her daughter into giving us up. I knew she was wrong.

"Krish, we have the same values, you and I," said Imma, raising her voice above the din. "You look after family, and so do I. Did I not help you get over your anxiety? Stay here and you'll never be anxious or fearful again."

A part of me was ashamed. She had helped me and been kind to me. But she was also holding us against our will to protect her village, and that was wrong. I ignored her and urged Dad to go faster.

One hundred feet.

"Not everyone is happy with this life, Imma," said Tashi, inching backward with us. "Lift the curse and let those who want to leave go. They have a right to live their lives the way they want."

"Foolish girl," said Imma. "There's nothing out there but chaos and greed. People wanting more and more till they destroy themselves and their world. You have nothing to compare it to, but trust me, you are not missing anything. Our ancestors suffered so we wouldn't have to."

"I want to decide that for myself," said Tashi.

Imma laughed. "You think these selfish, ungrateful people will look after you when you're a rat?"

Just as Tashi looked back to see our progress, Imma gave a piercing cry. The rats surged forward, leaping on Dad, on me, on Tashi. We batted them away with everything we had, but we were losing the battle. I was drowning in rats.

Suddenly, Rinchen leaped down from the birch, holding a branch aloft. He stuck it into the fire, and the dry wood caught immediately. He clambered up onto the pier just in time and swung it in an arc. The rats squealed and receded. It felt as if someone had lifted a boulder from my chest. We were back in the game.

"Untie the canoe," Rinchen said. "I'll hold them off. But you're taking me with you. I choose freedom as a rat instead of being stuck here as a human."

He swept the burning branch from side to side, keeping the tide of rats at bay while Tashi and I raced for the canoe, Dad crawling as fast as he could behind us.

I had no time to be afraid as I flung myself into the canoe, and I made it on the first try. It rocked dangerously but did not tip. Dad climbed in next with Tashi's help while I held the boat steady. Dad's jacket and shirt were shredded, and his chest and stomach were a bloody mess.

"Tashi, Rinchen, come on!" I called out. "Let's go!"

"No!" said Imma, lunging for Tashi. "You're making a huge mistake. Remember, no one can leave Imdur in human form. You're vermin to them, and they'll kill you. Neither of you stand a chance of getting to the city alive."

Tashi untied the second canoe and let it float away. She

started to untie the rope that tethered our canoe to the pier. Rinchen helped.

"Kill him!" Imma screamed. "Don't touch my daughter."

Five large Imdura, in rat form, jumped on Rinchen while his back was turned. They took him down. Tashi turned to help, but it was too late. One of the Imdura ripped Rinchen's throat out. He screamed and was silent. Forever.

They faced Tashi, twitching and drooling, as if she were a tasty morsel. Imma had only to nod her head and Tashi was a goner. Tashi knew it. With renewed strength, she untied the canoe. It shot away from the pier, in the grip of the current.

"Come on, Tashi!" I yelled. "Jump!"

Tears slid down her face. "I can't. You'll hate me if I do."

Shame washed over me again. She was and always had been the bigger person. She'd known I was using her but had helped me anyway. The canoe was moving faster now, but I couldn't leave without Tashi. She had saved us, and now it was my turn. To help her live her dream. I didn't care what form she took.

"I promised to look after you. Can you not trust me after I trusted you?"

Imma had crept up to Tashi while we'd been speaking and now stood beside her with burning red eyes. "You are the next shaman. You will not leave even if I have to kill you to keep you here." She clamped her hands around Tashi's neck, choking her.

Tashi gasped for breath, trying to get free.

"Throw her off!" I screamed. The boat was almost in the middle of the raging river. "*Jump!*"

Tashi bit her mother's hand. Imma shrieked and let go. Tashi plunged into the icy water and swam toward the boat.

"Dad, keep it steady," I said. I leaned over the side and yelled, "Faster!"

The current was strong, and the spray was bone-chilling. How would Tashi survive this? A few of the Imdura leaped into the water, giving chase.

"Faster!" I yelled, leaning as far out as I could, arm outstretched.

Tashi was level with the canoe. She reached out a hand. I grabbed it and hauled her up. Dad gripped my jacket and helped pull her in. Sodden and shivering, she climbed into the canoe between us. I started to take off my jacket, but she stopped me.

"Don't bother," she said. "It's almost time. Are you sure you won't break your promise when we get to Delhi?"

"You have my word," I said.

"You're the best thing that has ever happened to me, Krish." She leaned forward and planted a tiny kiss on my cheek.

"And you're the best thing that has ever happened to me," I said. "I'll keep you safe."

"One more thing," said Tashi. "It was I who bit you in the forest. Then Samya and her friends led you to the village where it would be safer from rogues like Rinchen. If you'd camped in the forest that night, you would not have survived to see the day."

My mind flashed back to the white rat, to when this all began. How scared I'd been at the time. *Look at me now.*

"Are you mad at me?" she said.

"That bite changed my life for the better and kept us alive," I said. "Thank you."

"Take me to the Taj Mahal, okay? That sketch you showed me was beautiful."

"I will."

"Krish, I need your help," said Dad as we rounded a bend in the river.

I moved to the center of the canoe and helped Dad navigate the narrow gorge. There was still quite a ways to go before we were safe.

"Krish, you had more sense in this adventure than I," Dad said. "If I'd respected the Imdura and their rules, we wouldn't be running for our lives with their shaman-to-be. I've been a stubborn fool, and I've broken up a family. Can you forgive me for not listening to you?"

"On one condition," I said. "That we never speak of this village or disclose its location to anyone. We have stolen something precious from them. We can't hurt them anymore."

"I agree with Krish," Tashi said. "Imma will be very sad that I am gone. And angry. Please do not talk of Imdur to anyone, or they will find us and kill us all." A tear, glowing silver in the moonlight, trickled down her cheek.

Dad turned around to look at us. "You have my promise."

When we'd navigated the turn, Dad and I paddling hard, I looked behind me. On the seat of the canoe was a small white rat with a red mark on its snout, shivering in the cold. I picked Tashi up. She squeaked and trembled.

"No one is following us," I said softly.

The river hurtled along toward Leh, the canoe firmly in her grip. Tashi had said it was about two hours to the city. How would we survive those two hours in the cold with no way to navigate except paddles? What if there were rapids or a waterfall? Had we come this far only to drown?

I thought about how weird this must be for Tashi, knowing she couldn't be human again unless she returned to Imdur. I stroked her nose and tucked her into my pocket. She trembled against my chest.

"Sleep now. You're safe with me." I patted my pocket gently.

An hour passed, and my arms were burning, trying to

keep the canoe steady as she whipped around corners in the swift current. Dad was slumped over the paddle, shaking with fever and exhaustion. Tashi couldn't help either.

Anjali, I wish you were here this minute. I could so use your help.

"Krish!" a voice called out from up ahead, around the bend of the speeding river.

Was I dreaming, or had I actually heard Anjali's voice?

"Dad!" I yelled. "Did you hear that?"

"I did," said Dad, rousing himself from his stupor.

The sight that greeted us made me want to laugh and cry. A motorboat strained against the current, chugging upstream. In the beam of the powerful lamps mounted on the boat, I picked out three people on board. My eyes locked with a small figure up front.

"Anjali!" I called out. "You came!" Words could not express the relief I felt.

"Krish, you're safe! Thank God!"

Her tone said it all. She still cared, and most importantly, she'd forgiven me.

"I have so much to tell you!" I yelled out as the boats swept closer.

"We have a lot to catch up on!" she called back.

I would apologize to her properly, and make it up to her,

when we got back home, but for now, just hearing her sound like her usual self was enough.

Dad, energized with the rescue so close at hand, worked with the camp staff to tether our boats together. They helped us climb on board and then cut loose the canoe. It bobbed away and capsized.

Anjali and I stood to one side while Dad created a story for the camp staff about our adventures without mentioning a word about Imdur or Imma.

"I was so worried about you when we lost contact," said Anjali. "I've been glued to the radio every second. I must have gone through dozens of batteries. And then when you called, I was so relieved." She threw her hands around me and hugged me tight. There was a sharp squeak, and she jumped back. "What was that?"

"Thanks, Anjali! You saved our lives. Dad's, mine, and Tashi's."

"Who is Tashi?" she said, staring at me with a strange expression.

I took the white rat from my pocket. "This is Tashi. She's the reason we're still alive. And the reason I'll never let you down again."

Tashi looked at Anjali with bright eyes. Anjali reached out a finger and stroked her gently. "She's cute."

"Yes, and she wants to see the Taj Mahal."

Anjali tucked a hand into mine. "We'll all go."

If someone had told me three days ago that Anjali and I would make up, and I'd be going home with a rat, I would have told them they were dreaming. My luck and life had changed, thanks to a bite from a white rat.

ACKNOWLEDGEMENTS

Thank you to my wonderful friends Deborah Kerbel, Helaine Becker, Frieda Wishinsky, and Michelle Mulder, who read early drafts of the manuscript and gave me valuable feedback. Thanks to the crew of the Writing Excuses Podcast (Mary Robinette Kowal, Brandon Sanderson, Howard Taylor, and Dan Wells), who've helped improve my craft. A special shout-out to Dan Wells, whose story structure is one of the best I've used. Love to my family, especially Rahul and Aftab. Thanks to my awesome agent, Naomi Davis, who believed in this story and in me. Finally, sincere thanks to my editor, Barry Jowett, who makes me a better writer with each story we work on.